SEAL'S PROPOSAL

TAKE NO PRISONERS

BOOK #5

ELLE JAMES

New York Times & *USA Today*
Bestselling Author

SEAL's *Proposal*

A Navy SEAL's plan to propose nearly ends in a snowy death in the Colorado Rockies

Remy LaDue, hot Navy SEAL with SEAL Team 10, is on a mission. He's planned a special vacation to the Colorado Rockies with the express purpose of proposing to the woman he loves on Christmas morning. He knows it's a long shot, with both their jobs keeping them away from each other for months out of the year, but he wants her as his forever lover and will risk everything to marry her.

Mitchell Sanders is as dedicated to her work as an NCIS agent as Remy is to his calling as a Navy SEAL. Independent, driven and passionate about justice and protecting innocents, she would no sooner give up her job as Remy.

When a criminal she helped to capture and convict escapes on the eve of their departure, Mitchell is torn between sticking around to recapture him and going with Remy, opting to follow her desire this once. Plans change as the mountains become a nightmare and they struggle to put an end to the threats that plague their idyllic vacation and Remy's plans for his

Christmas surprise.

From the Author

As a retired member of the armed forces, whose father was a career military man and whose sister and brother also served, I'd like to thank all the brave soldiers, sailors, airmen, SEALs, Coast Guard and special forces who are serving or have served and sacrificed to defend this great nation.

Please take the time to thank those who have served for their commitment and dedication to keeping us free and safe.

I'd like to dedicate this book to those who made the ultimate sacrifice of their lives and to the wounded warriors who so bravely face new challenges.

If you've enjoyed this story, please consider taking the time to leave a review on your favorite retail or reader review site. Authors appreciate your thoughts about the books you read and love it when you share them with others.

Enjoy!
Elle James
aka Myla Jackson

Chapter One

"GATOR. CHECK IT OUT. Bogey at ten o'clock, two hundred yards. You take him while I take the one on top of the east building."

Irish's voice filled Special Operations Chief Remy "Gator" LaDue's ear. He'd already spotted the man as he'd studied the mud-and-stick walls of the Afghan village. Through Remy's night vision goggles, a bright green heat signature glowed where the sentry stood guard near the main entrance of the walled village. "Got 'im." He took a breath of the cool, crisp air and held it as he stared through his night scope and zeroed in on the Taliban fighter, pinning him with an optical red dot.

The fighter's head dipped, and then rose to stare out at the night to see where the laser light originated. Before the man could react, Remy gently squeezed the trigger, sending a round through the fourteen-inch barrel of his suppressed H&K 416, at the same time as Irish fired on his target.

Thankfully, the Taliban fighter didn't yell an alert before his body slumped to the ground.

Remy shifted his sight immediately to the top of the east building in time to see the heat signature of a man drop to the dirt. He should have felt some regret over taking a life, but these men, the Taliban who'd taken over this village, had raped and killed a female U.S. soldier, and dumped her body in the desert with no regard for life, human rights or decency. They were ruthless terrorists whose leader was their main target that night.

Their mission was to annihilate the Taliban leader with minimal collateral damage.

"You two are making this look too easy." Fish moved up next to Remy's position next to a large boulder, his weapon at the ready.

His jaw tight, Remy nodded. "In and out. That's my aim for the night."

Irish chuckled softly. "Sounds like you're hooking up with your girl, not running a mission in the sandbox."

"Gator's gettin' hitched."

Fish's announcement came through the headset in Remy's helmet. His chest tightened and a niggle of fear swept through him. He hadn't let fear control him during BUD/S training as a Navy SEAL, or any of the thirty operations of which he'd been a part. But now... The one mission that meant more to him than any other in his life had him shaking in his combat boots. "Mitchell hasn't said 'yes,' *yet*."

"Have you asked?"

"No." He knew Mitchell loved him. The big question was, did she want to marry him? They'd been living together for ten months, ever since he'd come back on Valentine's Day to claim his pity date.

"What are you waiting on? Ask her already." Fish nudged him with his elbow.

"Unlike you bunch of dumb fucks, I want to do it right." While he spoke, he kept a close watch on the compound, searching for other guards while waiting for their team leader to make the call to breach the wall and take out the Taliban leaders who had entered the structure earlier that day. "I want to make it special."

"Do you have the ring?" Big Bird's deep voice sounded over the headset speakers.

"Big Bird's right," Irish said. "You know it's all about the ring."

Caesar Sanchez laughed softly. "Like you know what the hell you're talking about."

"I read books," Irish insisted.

"Fuckin' romance novels?" Caesar asked with a snicker.

"No." Irish paused, and then admitted, "Well, yes. It's like sneaking into enemy strongholds, collecting intel about what women like and don't like. A man can't be too well-armed."

Remy snorted. If anyone could be overly armed, it would be Irish. He liked his weapons, and he didn't mind carrying the extra weight into battle.

"Anyone know what the fuck 'radio silence' means?" Lieutenant Reed Tucker, Tuck, their team leader spoke quietly, but with authority, into the headset. "Irish and Gator, you're coming with me. Dustman, Nacho, and Big Bird, cover until we get to the wall."

Remy climbed to his feet, and then, hunkering low, he crept across the dry earth toward their target.

"Do you have the ring?" Caesar asked as Remy crossed the open space between the hills they'd been hiding behind and the village walls.

He didn't respond until he'd reached the wall without incident. "Really? You ask me if I got the ring when I'm in the fuckin' open?"

Irish low-crawled across the front wall to the opposite side of the entrance.

"What do you see?" Tuck asked, not responding to the chatter.

"Got one headed our way," Irish spoke in a clipped tone.

Remy peered around the corner of the gateway. A man in the traditional dress of the Afghan people walked toward him, carrying a not-so-traditional M4A1, probably pilfered from the body of an American soldier he'd killed.

Anger surged in Remy, but he held it in check, pulled his knife from the scabbard strapped to his thigh and waited for the man to cross the threshold of the gate. As soon as he spotted the armed man step through, Remy had him in a headlock and dispatched him, blood staining the sand around his feet.

Dragging him to the side, Remy dropped the dead man and joined Irish against the wall.

"Gate's clear," he said.

The rest of the men moved in while Irish and Remy covered, keeping a close watch on the road leading from inside the compound to the gate, should another guard or sleepwalking Taliban bastard decide tonight was his lucky night.

As he sat with one hand on the trigger, the butt of his weapon nestled against his shoulder, Remy lowered his other hand to pat the buttoned pocket on his pants leg where he'd tucked the ring box. Yeah, call him a stupid, sentimental fool, but, as added incentive to return to the States alive and well, he'd brought along the ring he planned on giving to Mitchell.

A movement in the village caught his attention, a door opened and a light flared in the lenses of his NVGs. A group of men exited one building and strode toward a truck. "We have movement," Remy warned the team.

"We're all here. Let's get this party started," Tuck replied.

The men standing in the narrow road paused to talk, some of them climbing into a truck.

Remy slipped around the side of the gate. Clinging to the dark sides of the buildings, staying out of the moonlight as much as he could, he crept forward, confident that Irish had his six.

"Let's light this place up," Tuck said.

Four more members of the team infiltrated the compound, sliding through the streets like snakes, clinging to the darkness, blending into the blackest shadows. Big Bird and Dustman remained outside the walls as backup, and to cover any incoming threats.

"Want me to take them?" Irish had a fully functional M79 launcher. One round would take out the truck and the people standing around. Any weapon they wanted, the Naval Special Warfare Group, DEVGRU, got it for them. One of the perks of being a SEAL.

"Let the truck go," Tuck said.

Firing a grenade into the mix would wake the entire village. They still needed to locate the Taliban leader and take him out. If they started the fireworks now, the leader would have the opportunity to slip out the back door, or sneak over the wall and escape. They couldn't let him go. The young female supply clerk he and his suck-ass subordinates had sexually molested and beheaded deserved justice. Shooting the bastard wouldn't be enough. Remy wanted to dismember him one limb at a time, starting with his dick. He was an animal to treat a woman like that.

Every time Remy thought of that young soldier, he couldn't help thinking about Mitchell. As an agent with the NCIS, she'd been in some tight undercover operations that could have gotten her killed or badly injured. A definite hazard of her position.

One that bugged the shit out of him. He didn't like that he couldn't protect her. But she wouldn't have it any other way. She prided herself in her ability to fight and defend herself. On numerous occasions, she'd told him she never wanted to rely on someone else to get her out of a tight spot. She had to escape on her own.

Remy understood her desire to be strong, but there was strong, and then there was team-strong. He'd learned through BUD/S training that no man was an island. You looked out for your buddy, and he looked out for you.

With Mitchell so damned determined to look out for herself, she'd never mentioned the "M" word. Marriage had never been part of their conversation. As much as he loved Mitchell, and he knew she loved him, Remy was afraid she'd turn down his proposal, refusing to marry him, viewing the arrangement as a sign of weakness. He had some convincing to do to persuade her that marrying him showed considerable strength. With the two of them dedicated to their jobs and no immediate desire to give them up, the decision would be a show of self-confidence and faith in each other to get married.

Or so he'd practiced in his speech. But the moment had to be right. He'd planned on popping the question while on their Christmas vacation in the Rockies. The only thing standing in his way of leaving for the trip was this mission, an operation they'd been planning since they'd received intel the Taliban leader was holed up in this village, holding its inhabitants hostage, threatening to kill the women and children should word that he was there leak out.

One brave old man, who'd seen more than his share of Taliban strong-arming and senseless murders, had left the village in the middle of the night and walked all the way to an American marine outpost to report on what was going on.

Within a matter of hours, the word was passed to all the right places. SEAL Team 10 had been given satellite photographs and been briefed on the buildings the Taliban had taken over.

The truck lumbered toward the SEALs' positions, and they fell back into the alleys and behind boxes or barrels, out of the direct beams of the dingy truck headlights. Once the truck was past, Remy moved closer.

The men who'd been standing outside reentered the nearby building, and the door closed behind them. A guard stood outside, an AK47 in his hands.

Irish took the lead, slipping up as close to the building as he could.

Remy tossed a pebble so it landed several yards farther into the village.

The sound jerked the guard's attention away from Irish's position for a moment.

That was all he needed. Irish lunged forward, grabbed the man by the throat and sliced a deep slash, hitting his carotid artery.

The man slumped to the ground, his eyes wide, staring blankly at the moon above.

Remy moved to the door, opened it and stepped into a narrow hallway. He switched to his MP7 submachine gun, a lighter, quieter weapon he normally used in close combat, especially when searching buildings from room to room. On the previous mission, Irish had killed a man with this weapon in one room, while the people in the next room never heard the shots fired.

Using the tip of his boot, Remy nudged open a door. A man lay on a pallet inside. With his knife, he took out the man without ever waking him.

Irish moved past Remy to the next doorway and waited for the team leader. Tuck moved into place, and with his weapon raised, Irish pushed open the door. The room was filled with cardboard boxes and wooden crates. A supply closet.

Remy hurried past to the next door, behind which he could hear voices. This had to be it.

Seeing Irish and Tuck were in position, Remy nudged the door open with his MP7. Seven men glanced his way with unsuspecting glances. Tuck and Irish opened fire, mowing down four of the seven men, their cries of surprise and pain reverberating around the room.

The other three dropped to the floor and hid behind boxes, firing at them with whatever weapon they had in hand.

Remy dove into the room, somersaulted, and came up firing. He hit one of the men only half-hidden behind a wooden crate. Another man aimed a rifle at him. Remy threw his knife, but not quickly enough.

The Taliban fighter's bullet clipped his thigh. A sharp twinge of pain burned across his skin, but didn't slow him down. Remy fired again, neutralizing the man with the gun, leaving only what appeared to be their target, cowering behind a crate.

Then the man stood, yelled something about Allah, pulled the pin on a grenade and lobbed it toward Remy.

Irish shot the Taliban leader as the grenade rolled to a stop at Remy's feet.

"Well, fuck." Remy bent, picked up the grenade and raced down the hall. He didn't know how long he had, but at least, he'd get the explosive away from his buddies. As he passed the room with the dead man on the pallet, he lobbed the grenade inside and closed the door, then threw himself to the ground, covering his ears.

An explosion shattered the wall beside him, slinging plaster, sticks, mud, and debris through the hallway. The concussion vibrated against Remy's eardrums, but he'd been fortunate to plug his ears before it happened. Still, a persistent whine filled his ears and blurred his vision.

Dust rose like a fog, choking off any visibility and filling Remy's lungs. He pulled his T-shirt up over his nose and staggered to his feet, brushing the crumbled stones and broken bits of wall from his shoulders.

"Gator?" Tuck's voice barked through Remy's headset.

"Still among the living," he answered, and coughed up a lungful of dust. "Did we get him?"

Tuck pushed past Remy, hand trailing on the

wall to feel his way toward the exit. "Target was eliminated. Got a positive ID and a color photo for a souvenir. Let's get out of here."

Unless they eliminated all potential threats, the exfiltration portion of a mission for the SEAL team was even more dangerous than infiltration. Now, the enemy had been alerted.

Tuck was first through the door, poised and ready.

Remy could already hear the pop, pop, popping of gunfire. Not until he emerged into the open night air did Remy feel the warm wetness of something dripping down his leg. Blood. A thought caught him in mid-stride, and he came to an abrupt halt, lowering his weapon for a moment to feel for his pocket. Maybe it hadn't been such a good idea—

A sharp report of a rifle and the whiff of a bullet winging past his ear made Remy drop to the ground and search the corners and rooftops for the sniper who'd almost plugged him in the head. Movement snagged his attention from the top corner of a low building, two structures away. Aiming through his rifle's sight, he waited. One thousand one. One thousand two.

A green heat signature at the top of one of the buildings lit up his NVGs.

The terrorist raised his rifle and fired. The bullet hit the ground beside Remy.

Unfazed, Remy steadied his hand, inhaled and caressed the trigger. The bullet left the chamber one second, and in the next, hit its target.

The man who'd been firing at Remy slid off the corner of the roof and hit the dirt at the base of the building.

"We got trouble coming," Big Bird said into the headset. "Two trucks full of Taliban headed for the village. ETA, five mikes."

Tuck spoke, "Time to blow this popsicle stand."

The plan was to leave the village as soon as they'd dispatched the target.

Remy followed Tuck and Irish through the tunnel-like streets toward the rear wall. A loud explosion shook the ground.

When Remy rounded a corner, he faced the back wall of the village, which now had a gaping hole where Dustman had created their escape route. Remy counted heads. The gang was all there, minus one. Big Bird, who had been the lookout at the entrance to the village.

With the entire village awake now, and two truckloads of angry Taliban heading their way, getting out wouldn't be a cakewalk.

Tuck was on the radio calling for their taxi. If all went according to plan, their ride would be there in less than two minutes. The group held their positions.

The thumping hum of rotor blades filled the air, and the two Black Hawks from the 160th Night Stalkers swooped in and hovered at the prescribed location on the north side of the village. Big Bird joined them, and they slipped through the crumbled wall and out into a poppy field. Gunfire erupted from one of the rooftops.

"Go!" Remy yelled and motioned his hand forward. "Fish and I will cover."

Fish took a position a couple yards from Remy, and together, they laid down suppressive fire while the rest of the team raced for the helicopter. Once they were safely on board, one of the helicopters lifted off, and the door gunner took over the job of keeping the enemy busy while Fish and Remy ran for the other chopper.

As the second Black Hawk left the ground, Fish dove in and Remy jumped in beside him, wincing when he bumped against his wounded leg. With everyone on board, they left the village behind.

The leading helicopter had circled back. From the open door of the Black Hawk, Remy watched as a missile launched from the other helicopter, hitting the first truck dead on. A fiery burst lit the sky as the two helicopters headed back to Camp Leatherneck.

Once they were out of range of RPGs, Remy could no longer ignore his own gunshot wound. He leaned forward, jammed his hand into his side pocket and cursed. "Damn."

"Were you hit?" Fish sat up beside him and pushed away his hands to check his injury.

"I'm fine. It's just a flesh wound."

"Is that all?" Fish snorted and pulled out a pressure bandage from one of his pockets, tore the fabric of Remy's trousers, and applied it to the torn flesh. "The way you were cussin', I thought it might be worse."

Remy pulled his hand out of the pocket of his trousers, the ring box in his grip. The exterior had been damaged, ripped open on the side where the bullet had hit the box before slicing his leg. He flipped the box all the way open and his heart fell.

The ring was gone.

"Fuck!" He dug his hand back into his pocket and fished around.

"Hey, will you let me finish dressing the wound?"

Remy shoved aside Fish's hands and dug deeper. When his fingers touched metal, Remy nearly fainted with relief. "Thank God."

Fish taped the dressing in place and clapped a hand on Remy's shoulder. "Thank God for what? Did you think you were going to die? Like you said, it was just a flesh wound. Your Cajun ass is gonna live."

Taking a deep breath, Remy laid back and pinched the bridge of his nose. "Maybe so, but I almost lost the goddamn ring."

Thirty-six hours later

If Mitchell Sanders could pace at that moment, she would have. Instead, she sat quietly in the Eastern District Court of Virginia in Norfolk. The trial had gone on for days, and finally, the jury had reached a decision. They would find Rocco Hatch guilty of four counts of murder and thirteen counts of human trafficking, including forcing a seventeen-year-old girl to have sex for money. They *had* to find him guilty and get him off the street for life. The man was evil, and should be put to death.

At least, that's how Mitchell felt. When she'd gone undercover to expose him, she hadn't realized just how many women's lives he'd ruined. Hatch and his partner Candy Sweeting were the lowest scum of the earth.

The members of the jury filed in and took their seats.

"Have the members of the jury come to a decision?" the U.S. District Court judge asked, his face drawn and tired.

A heavy-set man stood, holding a single piece of paper. "Yes, sir, we have. We, the members of the jury find Mr. Rocco Hatch guilty of all charges against him."

The spectators all let go of the breaths they'd been holding in heartfelt sighs and muttered praises to God. The judge closed the trial, and Rocco Hatch was led from the courtroom, his narrowed stare on Mitchell as he walked toward the door.

Mitchell stood, her gaze on the man who had wrecked the lives of so many women. *Good riddance.* Now, to get back to her own life. She had to pack and get ready for her first vacation in years, and the best part was that she was sharing it with the man she loved.

As Rocco neared the exit, he stopped and jerked free of the bailiff's hold. "Hey, Sanders! This isn't over." The man glared and shook his handcuffs.

The evil in his eyes so palpable it sent a shiver down Mitchell's spine. She left the courtroom more shaken than she should have been. The trial was just another event as an agent in the NCIS. She'd caught another criminal, and hopefully, the sentencing would put him behind bars for the rest of his douche-bag life.

Out in the parking lot, she drew in a deep breath of fresh air and tried to shake off a bad feeling, telling herself she shouldn't let Rocco's words get to her.

In less than two hours she'd be at her apartment, waiting for Remy's return. He'd texted as soon as his plane hit the ground in Norfolk. As usual, he couldn't come straight home. He had to go to his unit for the mission debrief, and then he'd be home. She'd have him back, safe and sound, in her arms and all would be right with the world again.

In her SUV, she unlocked the specially built safe in the console, removed her .40 caliber Glock from the compartment, and tucked it into the shoulder holster she wore beneath her black suit jacket. Comforted by the cold, hard steel, she shifted her vehicle into Drive and eased out of the parking lot onto the street.

A crowd still hovered around the door to the courthouse. As she came to a halt at the stop sign, she spotted Rocco as he exited the courthouse with his armed escorts.

The media mob swarmed him and the police officers as they edged toward the waiting police car.

For a moment, Mitchell lost sight of Rocco. Her pulse sped up and she craned her neck, searching the faces in the crowd for the bastard. Then he emerged, both cops still at his side.

While Mitchell had been searching for Rocco, she hadn't noticed the dark van speeding toward the group until it raced past her, jumped the curb, and plowed into a reporter and one of the police officers holding onto Rocco.

Women screamed and the crowd scattered.

Rocco butted his head into the other officer's nose so hard the man let go and grabbed his own face, blood streaming out between his fingers.

The van door slid open. Four men wearing ski masks and wielding automatic weapons jumped out and opened fire into the crowd, hitting the bleeding police officer and several others around Hatch. Those who could, took cover; those in the open either ran or hit the ground.

Hell no! Mitchell jammed her SUV into Park and dropped out of the vehicle, her gun drawn. Using the SUV as cover, she aimed at the nearest gunman and dropped him where he stood.

One of them grabbed Rocco and threw him

into the van. Another turned his weapon toward Mitchell and pelted her SUV in a wicked burst of bullets.

Mitchell hit the ground behind a tire, her pistol no match for the power and rapid delivery of an automatic. Still, she searched for any opportunity, aiming from beneath the SUV at their feet and fired again. She hit one in the foot.

But he managed to limp to the van along with the others. The door slid closed, and the driver sped away in a fog of scorched rubber.

The officers who'd taken cover behind the police car emerged into the street and fired at the van, but it was too late.

Rocco had escaped.

Mitchell rose from her position behind the SUV, her heart hammering against her ribs, a sick feeling filling her belly as Rocco's last words in the courtroom echoed in her mind.

This isn't over.

Chapter Two

"MITCHELL! I'M HOME!" Remy flung open the door to their apartment and dropped his duffel on the floor beside the entry. He cocked his head and listened. "Mitch?"

Stone-cold silence met him, not the excited rush of his warm, welcoming, soon-to-be-fiancée, slamming into him and wrapping her arms around his body. Perhaps she'd gotten caught up at her office.

He stared down at his watch. Wow, past seven o'clock. Past normal office hours. But then, when did the NCIS keep normal hours? Heck, when did SEALs? He checked his cell phone and found a text message from Mitchell.

Shit hit the fan at the courthouse, had to file a report. Will be home soon.

His disappointment faded. Mitchell was as dedicated to her job as he was to his. He couldn't fault her for that. But every once in a while, he wished they could be a normal couple and have more time to spend together. He was glad his commander had allowed him to schedule leave so far in advance. Making plane reservations could be troublesome when you didn't know if you'd be called out on an operation, or when you'd return.

He raised a hand to his chin and scratched at the scraggly beard that had grown over the last couple months. With time to kill, he could shit, shower, and shave, and be ready with dinner for when Mitchell came through the door. She'd be too tired to go out, and he really didn't want to. Remy would much rather have her to himself and catch up on all the lovemaking they'd missed while he'd been out of country.

Pushing aside the exhaustion of traveling halfway around the world in the back of a C130, he headed for the bathroom. An hour later, clean and his face scraped free of the beard, wearing a pair of cutoff sweat pants, Remy settled a pizza box on the counter and took out a slice. Cheese ran in a long string from the box to the wedge, the scent of fresh crust and tomato sauce making his stomach rumble.

Still, Mitchell hadn't appeared.

Too hungry to wait, Remy dove in and polished off four slices before he was satisfied.

His cell phone rang and his hand darted out to answer. He sighed. The caller ID indicated Irish.

"Hey, I just saw your fiancée on the news. Everything all right?"

Remy's pulse leapt. "Don't know. I'll get back to you." Dropping his phone on the couch, he dove for the television remote, clicking it on, and setting it on the local news station.

Images of the courthouse appeared on the screen, with gunmen and people scattering in all directions. In the background, he made out Mitchell's SUV. The image switched to a reporter pressing a microphone into Mitchell's face, asking her what had happened.

Mitchell's hair was pulled back into a ponytail and her face was grim. "No comment," she said, and pushed past the reporter, her body tense.

The news anchor droned on about Rocco Hatch's escape as Remy absorbed what had just happened. He was reaching for his cell phone when the scrape of a key in the lock caught his attention. Before the lock twisted, Remy was there, yanking open the door.

Mitchell stood in the frame, her face tired, the knees of her suit trousers ripped, and a smudge of dirt across her face. Her lips lifted. "Hey."

"Oh, baby." He opened his arms and she fell into them. He eased backward and closed the door behind her, gathering her against his body.

"You're a sight for sore eyes," she said, her words muffled against his naked chest.

Her breath was warm on his skin, stirring his blood. "Yeah, and you're not so bad yourself."

She snorted and pulled back enough to give him a crooked smile. "I had planned on being home hours ago, having a gourmet dinner cooked, and lying naked on the couch for when you walked through that door."

His cock twitched at the erotic image. "We can still do all that." He waved toward the kitchen counter. "I have an Italian gourmet dinner. Your favorite pizza pie with pepperoni, onion, and black olives." As he spoke, he slid her jacket over her shoulders and let it drop to the floor. Then he slipped the buckle of her shoulder holster loose, and eased it too from her shoulders, draping it over the back of a chair.

"Now you're talking." Mitchell skimmed her hands over his chest and around to his back, dropping low to capture his ass in her palms, pressing him closer. "Miss me much?"

Already hard, his member nudged her belly, ready to skip right to their reunion sex. With every ounce of control he could muster, he set her away from him. "You should eat. I need my woman to have the energy to last all night long. And tomorrow we're on our way to Colorado."

Her hands tightened on his buttocks and pulled him back against her. "I don't want food. I want you." Flashing a sexy grin, she leaned up on her toes and pressed her mouth against his.

His control unraveling, Remy's blood heated and he captured her head in his hands, slipping the ponytail free. God, it felt good to run his fingers through her hair, and to feel her body pressed against his.

The tight buds of her distended nipples scraped his chest through her shirt and bra, and he couldn't wait to get her out of her clothes.

Sucking in a breath, Mitchell slipped her hands inside the elastic of his shorts and gripped his naked butt. "Aren't we a bit overdressed?"

"Absolutely." He leaned away and plucked at the buttons on her blouse, popped a few as he worked his way down the front and pulled the hem free of her trousers.

She shoved his sweat shorts over his hips and down his legs, skimming over his bullet wound.

He ignored the sharp stab of pain and tore her shirt off her back, flinging it against the wall.

"What's this?" She backed away and stared at the long gash along his thigh that had been neatly stitched by one of the docs at Camp Leatherneck.

He shrugged. "Just a flesh wound." Eyeing her bared skin, he tried to pull her back into his arms.

With a hand planted on his chest, she resisted.

"We shouldn't be doing this. You're wounded." Her brows furrowed. "Shrapnel or gunshot wound?"

"Gunshot." He smiled.

Her lips pressed together, and she shifted her gaze from the wound to his face. "Everyone else okay?"

"We all made it back safely."

She stared for a moment longer before laying her cheek against his chest and wrapping her arms around his waist. "I know I'm not supposed to, but I worry so much when you're away on an operation."

He liked that she cared, but not that she worried. "Goes both ways." He smoothed his hand over her soft hair and tipped up her face. "Seems you had a little excitement today."

"Can we not talk about that right now?" Her lips clamped tight.

"Sure. What would you like to do? Eat pizza, make love, get a shower?"

A chuckle shook her. "Yes to all of them, but not in that order. Shower first." She stepped away and stared at his naked body. "Too bad, you've already had yours."

"I've been in the desert for a month. I'm sure I missed a spot or two. A man can never be too clean." He loved that no matter how tough she was, she was all soft and feminine when it counted. In the bed and in the shower, those attributes counted.

He reached for the button on her trousers, freed it, and dragged the zipper down the front. The fabric glided down her legs, pooling at her ankles.

She kicked her feet free and stood in her bra and panties. "It's a start, but we're not in the shower yet, and I'm covered in road grime."

Road grime. The word reminded him of the scene on the TV. He opened his mouth to say something about what had happened.

Before he could, she touched a finger to his lips. "Let's not talk about work. I want it to be just you, me, water and soap. I like it when we get all slippery." She took his hand in hers and led him into the bathroom where her bra and panties were quickly discarded.

Remy twisted the handle on the shower and set the water temperature to a comfortable level, then leaned down and scooped up Mitchell, wrapping her legs around his waist. He kissed her, his tongue slipping past her teeth to slide the length of hers. He could spend the rest of his life kissing and making love to this woman. She was everything he'd ever dreamed of, and more.

Stepping over the edge of the tub, he turned her back to the shower and let the warm water run over her body and between them. Steam rose around them, filling the air. Lowering her feet to the ground, he squirted a healthy dose of scented body wash into his hands.

Starting at her shoulders, he built a lather, and then traveled downward to smooth over her beautiful breasts. The feel of her skin under his touch kicked up his pulse. "I missed these," he said, bent to capture a taut nipple between his lips and sucked it into his mouth.

"Really? You missed my breasts?" She laughed and plumped the one he feasted on, encouraging him to take more into his mouth. "I have to admit, the girls missed you, too."

Loving the sound of that, he nipped the tip.

Mitchell sucked in a sharp breath. "Hey. They're for tasting, not eating." She wove her fingers through his hair and cupped the back of his neck, guiding him to the other nipple, while she slid her leg up the back of his.

He loved it when she gave as good as she got. The woman was fierce in her job and in the bed, and he couldn't believe she wanted to be with him. He couldn't wait to pop the question and make their claim on each other official.

As he tugged, sucked, and nibbled at her breast, he felt her body tense.

"Is it hot in here, or is it me?" She gripped his ears and dragged him up. "Enough foreplay. Tell me you have protection."

Through narrowed eyes, he stared at her flushed face. "You aren't there yet."

She cupped his balls and squeezed gently. "I'll be all over there, if you don't get a condom and get inside me now. I want you. We can worry about the foreplay later."

Remy grinned. "Where's the romance?"

She stomped her foot, splashing water over the side of the tub. "Goddamn it, Remy! Either you want me, or you don't. If I don't have you inside me in the next ten seconds, I'll come completely apart at the seams." She captured his face in her hands and forced him to look into her eyes. Then she kissed him hard, while running a hand over his long, thick, and incredibly hard shaft.

"A guy likes a little romance," he grumbled.

"Bullshit." She rubbed her thatch of hair over his cock.

It twitched in response.

"Fortunately," he said, reaching for the condom he'd staged behind the shampoo bottle, "a good SEAL always comes prepared." He held it up with a grin.

"Thank God." She ripped the foil packet from his hands, tore it open, and rolled it down over his engorged staff. "Now, Mr. Navy frogman. Take me. And make it hard and fast." Mitchell entwined her arms around his neck.

Remy scooped her up, and she wrapped her legs around his waist. He backed her against the cool tile of the shower wall, felt her momentary flinch, and drove into her hot, wet channel. She hadn't been lying about being ready, so slick with her juices.

"Is that all you got?" she taunted. "Show me how tough you are. Give it to me."

"You got it, sweetheart." He dragged her hands above her head and pinned them with one of his big paws. Then he slammed into her, holding her hip, pressing her firmly against the shower wall. Like the other times, he marveled at the feel of their bodies and how they fitted tight. He pumped in and out, faster and faster, his body tightening with each thrust, the tension building inside until it bunched into a dense concentration. One more thrust into her, his member sliding through the heat, and his insides exploded outward in a burst of energy, sending electricity from his core all the way out to his fingertips. He let go of her wrists and held her hips in both hands, buried as deeply as he could go. For a long time, he stayed there, his cock pulsing, his body shaking with the intensity of their connection.

When at last he could think with his head, not his dick, he lifted her off him and stood her on her feet. "We're not done yet."

"Good." She flashed him a grin. "I bought new sheets, and I haven't slept on them naked yet. I wanted to break them in with you."

Remy burst out laughing. "For a badass female, I'd say that was the most feminine thing I've heard you say." He slapped her ass and handed her the soap. "I'll wash your hair while you finish up. And don't take too long, I'm curious about how those sheets will feel against my skin. Then, when you're good and fucked, you can tell me about your day."

"That's going to be a while. I want to make up for the month you've been gone, and I don't want to spoil the experience by talking about work."

"We frogmen have ways of making people talk." He bent and tongued the curve of her neck.

"Yeah, I believe you do." She sighed and leaned back against him. "Fine. I'll talk, but *after* we check out the sheets."

An hour later, Mitchell lay in the curve of Remy's arms, tired, but not sleepy, satiated for the moment, but willing to do it again at the slightest nudge. In the midst of her happiness that Remy was home and safe, she couldn't ignore the threatening pall of darkness from intruding on her joyful reunion with the man she loved.

"Okay, sweetheart, you've worn me out. All I can do is lie here and listen." He pulled her against him, an arm wrapped around her shoulder, his hand dangling over her nipple, teasing it into a tight bud. "Tell me what happened."

Drawing a deep breath, Mitchell started out slowly, describing the trial, the testimony from the victims and the remorseless expression on Rocco's face. She went on to tell him about the crowd outside the courtroom, the van and the attack. She skipped over the part where Rocco directed his parting remark toward her as he left the courtroom. Why worry Remy, when he'd just gotten home from a much more dangerous mission? She moved against his side. "I'm not hurting your wound, am I?"

"Holy shit, Mitch. I'm fine." His grip tightened. "But you could have been killed."

She rested a hand on his chest. "I wasn't even close."

Remy lifted her chin. "The hell you weren't. I saw the film clip."

"I'm fine. That's what matters." She sighed. "He escaped, Remy. All that work to put him away for good and he fucking slipped through our fingers."

"I'm more concerned about you." He pulled her closer. "Rocco is a psychopath. From what I've read about him, he's ruthless and vindictive.

During that entire trial, did Rocco give you any indication he blamed you for busting up his operation and getting him thrown in the slammer?"

Trust Remy to get to the center of her concern. "Well, as a matter of fact..."

"Damn." Remy leaned up on his elbow and stared down, his brow pulled into a frown. "That bastard is loose. What are the chances he'll come after you?"

"Slim?" she replied, without conviction.

From the look in Remy's eyes, he wasn't buying her answer either. "Good thing we're getting out of town tomorrow afternoon."

She touched his chest with the tip of her finger. "About that..."

He captured her finger in his hand. "We're getting out of town."

"I probably need to stay and help the police and the NCIS find Rocco."

"No way." He jerked upright. "We've been planning this trip for months. I've had to sell my soul to Gunny and the LT to get the time off. We're going. And I can't think of a better way to get you out of range of that nut job than to take you halfway across the country."

Mitchell chewed on her lip. The agent in her wanted to stay and put a stop to the psychopath. The woman in love wanted to please the man she cared about. Even if she stayed and worked the case, it could be a long time before they found Rocco. If he was smart, he'd get the hell out of town and lay low until the smoke cleared. Considering the men who'd sprung him had killed a cop and two reporters, she doubted the local police and the NCIS needed one more person on the manhunt.

Cop killers were raw meat to law enforcement personnel. They'd be rabid to find Rocco, and the men who'd freed him.

"Okay, we'll go."

Remy let go of the breath he'd held and grinned. "Good." Dropping a light kiss on her forehead, he laid down beside her and drew her into his arms, his entire body relaxing against hers. "You won't regret it. I think you'll like my Christmas present." With a yawn, he closed his eyes and nestled deeper into the mattress. "At least, I hope you do," he muttered. "I put a lot of thought into it."

From worry about Rocco to one more thing to worry about. Mitchell lay in the shadows, the moonlight taking the edge off the darkness, and stared up at the ceiling. When had Remy had time to go Christmas shopping for her? Hell, she had been stateside all this time and hadn't even set a foot into a store. Well, damn. She'd have to wait until they got to the ski resort and find something there.

Having never been in a committed relationship through a Christmas holiday, she had completely forgotten that a gift exchange was expected. She hoped he hadn't spent much on her. Hell, since he'd just gotten back from a deployment, he hadn't had time to shop. He had to have been thinking about it long before he left. What guy thought about Christmas presents in October?

She turned toward Remy. He lay against the new sherbet-pink sheets. His dark skin and hair had been a sharp contrast to the ultra-feminine color, accentuating his masculinity. He'd teased her about lying in a bed that reminded him of cotton candy, but it hadn't stripped him of any of his manliness. Broad shoulders, bulky biceps, and taut abs spoke of a man who prided himself on keeping fit for battle.

He'd come from a loving family who spent time together at Christmas. Whenever he spoke of his mother, he smiled. Of course, he'd think about gifts at Christmas time. With a mother he loved guiding him through the niceties of family life, he'd remember.

Mitchell sighed. Her own mother had died of breast cancer when she was nine. Her father had been so distraught by her passing that he'd barely spent time with Mitchell. On the rare occasion, he'd take her fishing or hunting. But he didn't remember birthdays, and Christmas reminded him too much of her mother. More than once, Mitchell assured him the holiday didn't mean anything to her, and that she didn't mind when he forgot to give her gifts.

After losing her first fiancé to the war in the gulf, she'd almost given up on love and relationships. Until Remy had stepped in to comfort her in the hours after her fiancé's funeral.

Boy, had that been a mess. They'd hooked up that night, before the ground Derek was buried in had time to settle. It took a year for her to forgive herself for falling in bed with his best friend only days after Derek's death.

Since then, she knew in her heart that Derek would have been happy for her. Remy was the type of man she needed in her life. A man who understood her desire to work for the NCIS, the danger she faced and her need to be independent. He wouldn't ask more of her than she was willing to give. And she wouldn't expect more. Status quo was good. She snuggled against his side and inhaled the scent of soap and male. Life couldn't get better.

Well, one aspect could get less complicated— if the police or NCIS rounded up the escaped Rocco.

Either way, she wouldn't let anything stand in the way of enjoying her vacation with Remy.

Chapter Three

MITCHELL EXITED the bathroom after conducting her morning routine. She'd tried to rise without waking Remy and thought she'd succeeded, until she opened the bathroom door and found him dressed in jeans, a T-shirt and a black leather jacket. "Where are you going?"

"To my unit. I have to report in today, even if just for an hour. Gunny and the LT wanted to go over the debrief one more time before I left and forgot the details." His lips twisted. "They said something about too much sex making you lose brain cells."

She tossed a towel at his head. "Great. So you talk to your buddies about our sex life?"

"No, *they* talk to *me* about our sex life." He chuckled. "They think I need advice and aren't hesitant in the least to give it." He reached out and pulled her into his arms. "They are jealous because I have one, and they don't."

"Oh, surely Tuck, Nacho and Fish aren't jealous. They have lovely ladies in their lives."

"Yeah, it's not them. It's the guys who are currently unattached."

"Those guys need women."

He lifted an eyebrow and cocked his head.

"Are you volunteering to play matchmaker?"

She snorted. "Do I look like the matchmaker type?"

"When you were pole dancing undercover at Rocco's place, you could have fooled anyone."

"Yeah, well, the boys won't get to see me dance again." She traced a line along his jaw to his lips. "The only person I dance for now…is you."

He kissed her, tracing his own lines along the length of her tongue to the tip and back, while he rubbed his body against hers.

Mitchell's insides revved and her blood burned hot through her veins. "If I didn't have to go to the office…" she whispered into his mouth.

Remy lifted his head and frowned. "I thought you were off all day."

"I was. But I want to check in on the hunt for Rocco."

"Couldn't you do that with a phone call?"

"I could, but I want to know how they're handling it." She smoothed a finger along his jaw. "Sometimes they don't tell me everything over the phone."

"I don't like the idea of you running around town with a killer on the loose." He kissed the tip of her nose and each of her cheeks. "Especially one who more-or-less threatened you."

"I'll be okay. It's daytime, and no one would do anything in broad daylight."

"Uh, darlin'…" He eased her backward to arms' length. "In case you hit your head and don't remember, the attack yesterday happened in

35

broad daylight."

That was true. She fought from displaying that sentiment in her expression. "Yeah, but surely they won't try something that stupid two days in a row. I mean, really. Is killing me so important that he'd risk getting caught again?"

Remy's answer was to pull her into his arms and hold her tight. "Sometimes, I wish you didn't work for the NCIS."

Hearing his caring tone touched her, and she laughed softly. "Sometimes, I wish you weren't a SEAL. So, we're even."

With a sigh, Remy let go of her. "Just don't be out all day. We have to get packed and to the airport two hours early."

"I'll be ready." She kissed him one more time, slipped into her jacket, grabbed her purse and left the apartment.

She'd just reached the parking lot and was about to cross it when a trash truck backed away from the huge bin it had just emptied. Rather than hurrying across, Mitchell stepped back, even with the bumpers of the cars parked on either side of her.

The garbage truck picked up speed, still backing up. A brief thought crossed Mitchell's mind that the driver was being reckless to go so fast in a parking lot. Sometimes, small children darted out from between cars.

She drew in a deep breath to shout at the driver to slow down when the truck's rear end swerved, heading directly for her. Caught off guard, she froze, a full second passing before she realized that if she didn't move, she'd be hit. Spinning, she ran back the other way.

The crunch of metal on metal and squealing tires filled the air.

A glance over her shoulder made her heart slam into her ribs. The two vehicles she'd stood beside were sliding sideways and almost on her heels.

She picked up her knees and elbows and ran faster, ducking into the stairwell she'd just exited. The cars slammed into the side of the building—the brick walls the only things keeping the crushed vehicles from hitting her.

From the stairs above, Remy leaped, landing on the ground beside her. "What the hell?"

Gulping for air, Mitchell pointed at the cars blocking their exit. "That garbage truck," she gasped. "It almost hit me." Now that the cars were no longer chasing her, she pulled her gun from her shoulder harness and threw herself across the nearest car.

"Where the hell do you think you're going?" Remy yelled, grabbing at a foot.

She shouted over her shoulder, "That was no accident." Mitchell left Remy in the stairwell and ran after the garbage truck turning onto the street at the end of the parking lot.

The garbage truck raced out into traffic. A driver slammed on his brakes and skidded to a halt, narrowly missing the truck. His quick stop caused the guy behind him to ram into his rear end, pushing him into the backside of the truck. The garbage truck didn't slow or stop, but sped away.

Remy caught up with Mitchell at the main road as she raised her handgun, pointing it at the truck.

He gripped her arm. "Don't shoot."

"He nearly killed me."

"The bullet could ricochet off the heavy metal and hit an innocent."

Of course, he was right. She lowered her gun and would have taken off running after the truck if Remy hadn't tightened his hold on her arm.

"You won't catch him on foot, Mitchell." He tugged gently, easing her back from the edge of the road. "We need to call it in and get the police after him."

"Damn!" Mitchell jammed her weapon into the holster beneath her jacket.

Remy yanked his cell phone out of his pocket and hit 9-1-1. "Did you see the driver's face?"

"Hell, no." Mitchell shoved a hand through her hair and then reached for her own phone. "I was too busy getting my ass out of the way before it was crushed."

Remy reported the incident to the police, and Mitchell called her boss at the NCIS.

"Damn, Mitchell," Patrick Holzhaus's gravelly voice rumbled into her receiver. "I can't let you out of my sight for a minute without you getting in trouble."

"Trust me, I wasn't asking for it." She turned

to stare at the two small cars smashed into the side of the building. "Getting to the office this morning might take me longer than I'd anticipated."

"Why are you coming in at all? I thought you were on vacation."

"I wanted to know what's going on. What's the status of the search for Rocco?"

"We're following leads, but so far, they're coming up empty."

Frustration made her pace a couple feet away. "Did you check with his family?"

"Done. No one's talking, and we got special warrants issued to search their premises." Patrick paused. "Nothing."

"What about DD's corral? Could he have gone back to his nightclub?"

Patrick laughed. "He'd be a fool if he did."

"The man *is* a fool. An insane fool," Mitchell reminded him.

Beside her, Remy was describing to the emergency dispatcher what had happened and what had been damaged.

"Sanders," her boss said, "the NCIS, local police and the state police are all looking for Rocco. We know the routine. We'll get him."

"He's dangerous, and he has people who will do his dirty work for him, as evidenced by this most recent attack." Her stomach tightened and her breath hitched. "And apparently, they know where I live."

"All the more reason for you to stay away

from the office, go on vacation, get out of the state and relax. We'll handle it."

"But—"

"No buts," her boss stated with finality. "Have a good vacation. That's an order."

The line went dead, and Mitchell tucked her phone into her pocket as Remy ended his call. "Guess we're stuck here for at least an hour answering questions."

"I'll stay and handle it." Mitchell waved toward the approaching police cruiser, its sirens blaring. "You can go on to your unit."

"While you were talking to your boss, I called and told the LT I'd be in later."

"Did you happen to tell the dispatch that the man was driving a big-ass garbage truck? It's kind-of hard to miss." Mitchell shook her head as the police car pulled into the parking lot next to them.

The cop got out of the car and addressed Remy. "Are you the guy who reported the accident?" The officer looked past Remy to the mangled cars smashed up against the apartment building. Residents had gathered on the pavement around the vehicles, talking to each other, their eyes wide, curious.

A woman came down the stairs in the blocked stairwell, her brows descending. "My car!" She clapped a hand to her cheek and shook her head. "What happened to my car?"

"Here we go," Mitchell muttered, and then turned to the policeman. "Did dispatch send someone after the garbage truck?"

The cop finally looked at Mitchell. "It was reported abandoned in the middle of the road one mile south. It's blocking both lanes and causing a traffic jam. Units are on scene."

"Sweet Jesus." Mitchell shook her head. "Are you telling me you're more worried about the traffic jam than capturing a man who came within one foot of murdering someone?"

"Of course not." The man shook his head. "Are you the victim of the attack?"

Mitchell planted her hands on her hips. "Damn right, I am."

"Sorry, ma'am." The cop had the audacity to smirk. "What I heard was that by the time the police got to the garbage truck, the driver was long gone."

A frustrating hour and at least one hundred questions answered later, tow trucks arrived and hauled away the totaled cars. The policeman who'd taken the report had left, and the rubber-neckers had dispersed.

"Want to go to my unit with me?" Remy asked.

Mitchell shook her head. "No. I need to pack."

Remy glanced at his watch. "As much as I hate to, I still need to swing by the unit. I'll be home in an hour and a half. I'll need only fifteen minutes to pack, and we can hit the airport at least an hour and a half early for our flight."

"Good." She leaned up on her toes and pressed a kiss to his lips. "I'll see you in a few."

She turned and walked away, but Remy stayed right with her. "Don't you have to go to the office?" she asked, annoyed that he was still there.

"Yes. But I'll go as soon as I see you safely to the apartment."

"I'm fine. I have my Glock." She patted it, liking the reassurance of the solid weapon against her ribs.

"Yeah. A Glock didn't help you much against a garbage truck."

"Only because I wasn't expecting to be run over by a truck."

"Now that you know someone is after you, you need to maintain situational awareness."

"You're preaching to the choir, sweetheart, and pissing me off." She gave him a shove toward his SUV. "Go. I'll be fine. I'm a big girl and can take care of myself."

They'd reached the stairwell leading up to their apartment.

"Okay. But lock the door, and don't open it for anyone but me."

"I have my gun, for Pete's sake."

"What if they show up with the same automatic weapons they used at the courthouse?"

Damn the man. "I hate it when you have a good point." She kissed him hard and ran up the stairs. "I'll be ready when you get back. So, hurry."

He crossed his arms and frowned. "Maybe I should stay."

Mitchell ground to a halt and glared at him. "Get the hell out of here or we'll miss our plane." She turned her back on him and entered her apartment, closed the door behind her, locked it, and then hit the light switch.

Nothing.

With plenty of light filtering into the room around the faux wood blinds, she could make her way around the apartment as she tried another light switch. Again. Nothing.

"What the hell?" That creepy feeling of impending doom settled in the pit of her belly as she tried several more light switches before concluding her electricity wasn't working. She went to the breaker box and shined her phone's flashlight into it. All the breakers were on, along with the master switch.

Mitchell scrolled through her contacts list for the apartment manager's number. It took six rings before he answered.

"Hello."

"Is this the apartment manager?" she asked.

"It is."

She gave him her apartment number. "My electricity is out."

"Did you pay your bill?"

"Hell yes."

"No one else is experiencing an electrical outage. I'll send over the maintenance man, but I suggest you also put a call in to the power company."

When Mitchell got off the phone with the

apartment manager, she searched the internet for the service number for the local electric company and was promptly put on hold. "I can't fucking believe this."

As she waited for a customer service representative to answer, she used a flashlight to find her way through her apartment. She dragged a suitcase out from the closet and plunked it on top of the bed. Five minutes on hold and she had all the undergarments she'd need for a week in the mountains packed. Ten minutes on hold and shirts, sweats and a sexy baby doll nightgown were folded neatly beside her undergarments.

At fifteen minutes, she had her toiletries, trousers, thermal underwear, gloves and goggles packed. All she needed was her waterproof winter jacket and she was ready to go. Twenty minutes and someone finally answered the phone. "How may I help you?"

"My electricity is out." Mitchell gave him her address and waited.

"I'm sorry, ma'am, but I show a call was made late yesterday evening by a Ms. Mitchell Sanders, asking that the electricity be cut off today. The note on the order says the customer was moving."

Too weird. "I'm obviously not moving, and I didn't call anyone yesterday to cut off the electricity."

"I'm sorry, ma'am, it's in our records. Are you Ms. Mitchell Sanders?" He rattled off her name, address and personal cell phone number.

"I am."

"The name, address and telephone number match on the work order," the rep insisted.

A creepy feeling settled in her gut. "Well, it wasn't me. How soon can I have my electricity turned back on?"

"I'm sorry, ma'am, the service technician won't be back in your area until tomorrow."

"You're kidding me, right?"

"No, ma'am. It'll be tomorrow before you have electricity to your house."

"Un-fucking-believable."

"Do you want your electricity reconnected, ma'am?"

"Damn right, I do. Today. Now." After confirming once again that the electricity would be turned on the next day, Mitchell opened the blinds to let in as much light as possible. Thank goodness, they were leaving that afternoon. Going without electricity for twenty-four hours was a freakin' pain in the ass.

Mitchell's cell phone beeped with the sound she used for text messages. Thinking it might be Remy, she hurried to check.

The text screen had just blinked off when she reached for it. She hit the on button, and the screen displayed a message that made her blood run cold and her heart skip several beats.

DIE BITCH!

As she stared down at the screen, the phone rang and she fumbled with it, almost dropping it on the tile floor. Catching it just in time, she read the caller ID.

Blocked Number

Reluctant to answer, but getting angrier by the minute, she hit the talk button. "Hello."

"No one fucks with me and gets away with it," the deep voice said.

"Rocco, you sick bastard, turn yourself in now," Mitchell said, her hand clamped tightly to the cell phone, her voice shaking with rage. "Because if I find you, I'll shoot your ass. You won't get a second chance in court."

"You can't shoot me if I kill you first." The line went dead.

For a moment, rage consumed Mitchell, and she wanted to throw the cell phone against the wall. But the phone rang again.

This time, the caller ID was Remy LaDue. With her hand half-cocked to throw, she retracted it and pressed the talk button. "Thank God," she said in a rush.

"What's wrong?" Remy asked.

Pulling herself together, Mitchell inhaled, let it out, and then answered. "Nothing, except the electricity is out."

"Power outage?" he asked. "We aren't having a storm."

Rather than worry him unnecessarily, she

lied. "Maybe the garbage truck hit a power pole."

"Maybe. Just keep the door locked and your gun ready. Key in 9-1-1 and be ready for anything."

"I'm fine. I even managed to pack in the dark."

"Good." A muted voice sounded in the background. "Look, I have to go, but I'll be home in less than an hour."

After Remy rang off, another text message flashed across the screen.

A LOT COULD HAPPEN IN AN HOUR

Her breath hitched in her throat. How did Rocco know it would be an hour before Remy returned? Or was it just coincidence that he mentioned an hour?

Feeling like a big weenie, Mitchell dialed 9-1-1. She gave her name and reminded the dispatcher of the garbage truck incident earlier.

"How can I help you, Ms. Sanders?"

"I thought I saw the driver of the truck again, lurking in the parking lot."

"I can have a unit sent to patrol the area."

"Thanks. I'd appreciate it." When she ended the call, she wasn't surprised when another text message flashed across her screen.

THE COPS WERE NO HELP AT THE COURTHOUSE

"Bastard." Mitchell called the phone company and reported her phone number had been hijacked, and someone was listening in on her conversations.

"We could send you a new phone."

"And how long would that take?"

"It could be to you in two business days' time."

"Never mind."

A beep sounded, and another message displayed across her screen.

BANG! BANG! YOU'RE DEAD!

Mitchell dropped her phone on the hard tile floor of the kitchen and ground her heel into the screen. As soon as she destroyed the device, she regretted the action. "Well, shit." If she needed to call the police, now she had no way of doing it.

For the next hour she sat in the dark, no television, no radio to listen to, and her phone was well and truly dead.

By the time Remy returned to the apartment, she was ready to climb the walls.

Rocco wanted her, and she was more than ready to take him on.

Chapter Four

REMY TRIED five times to call Mitchell's cell phone. Twice from the unit, and three more times on his drive home. As he drove the streets of Virginia Beach, all manners of scenarios had run through his mind. None of them good.

If anyone harmed a hair on Mitchell's head, he'd kill him, ripping his limbs off one at a time. The more he thought about someone hurting Mitchell, the heavier his foot pressed on the accelerator, until he was speeding twenty and thirty miles per hour over the posted limits. He ran two red lights and almost T-boned a minivan before he forced himself to slow and take a deep breath.

She would be fine. He'd find out the electricity had been restored and she was just in the shower, unable to hear the phone ringing. Rocco wouldn't have made his move on her. He wouldn't have been watching her apartment all this time, waiting until she'd been left alone.

Once again, he slammed his foot on the accelerator and wove through traffic, dodging pedestrians and bicycles.

When he reached the apartment complex, he didn't bother to park between the lines. Instead, he skidded to a stop so fast, he bumped up against the curb. Not giving a damn about his SUV's wheel alignment, he threw it into Park and leaped out. He took the steps two at a time, arriving at the apartment door, breathing hard. Too worried to wait until he fished his key out of his pocket, he banged a fist on the wooden door. "Mitchell! It's me, Remy. Let me in."

She didn't answer immediately, and he banged again, at the same time as he shoved his key in the lock. As he turned the key, the door yanked open and Mitchell stood there, a sheepish smile on her face. "Where's the fire?"

He pushed through the door, grabbed her in his arms, and kicked the door shut with his foot. "Why the hell didn't you answer your phone?"

She lifted her hand, showing him the broken phone. "Would you believe I dropped it?"

All the tension left him in a rush, and he gathered her against his body, holding her so tight he thought he might break her. "I was so scared."

"I told you—"

"I know. I know. You're fine. You have your gun." His heart rate returned to normal, but he couldn't relax his hold.

"Yes, I do." She snuggled into his shirt, her fingers curling around the fabric. "But I have to admit, I'm glad to see you."

"Oh, baby. I can't wait to get out of here and on our way to Colorado."

"Me too."

He laughed, the sound shaky, even to his

own ears. "I thought you didn't want to go."

"A girl has the right to change her mind."

"Good." He lifted an eyebrow. "What say you and I get to the airport early?"

"I'm with you. But you need to pack."

"Five minutes, tops, and I'll be ready to go." He snatched the duffel bag he'd left by the door and carried it through to the bedroom.

"Do you mind if I borrow your phone?" she asked, following.

"Not at all." He dug it out of his back pocket and handed it to her.

She left him alone in the bedroom, which suited him just fine. The only thing he needed from the duffel bag was the ruined jewelry store box with the diamond engagement ring nestled against torn velvet inside. He'd used medical tape to strap the ring box together while he'd laid on a gurney getting his leg stitched. At first, the doc hadn't wanted to waste good medical tape, but when he'd seen that Remy had an engagement ring inside, he'd handed him the tape himself.

It looked like hell on the outside, but maybe Mitchell wouldn't care, as long as what was on the inside meant something.

He could hear her voice in the next room as he dug into the duffel bag and removed his shaving kit, the ring box tucked in one of the pouches. One at a time, he felt in the mesh sections until he found the box and pulled it out.

Mitchell paced past the door at that exact moment, peering in while she reported to her boss in hushed tones.

Remy couldn't quite make out the words, and figured she was trying to be quiet so as not to disturb him while he packed. Once she'd moved past the open door and out of sight again, he slid the box into his pocket and stood. Fishing an empty suitcase out from under the bed, he laid in shorts, long underwear, socks, shirts and sweats. He topped that with outerwear for skiing to include insulated gloves, a black knit cap, goggles, snow pants and an insulated ski jacket.

They'd rent skis, helmets, boots and poles at the resort. He packed one dressy outfit consisting of black trousers, a black tailored shirt, gray tie and black sports coat. He wanted to take her out to one of the nicer resort restaurants and woo her by candlelight, saying sweet nothings that would butter her up for the Christmas morning surprise. Every word of love and commitment would be one-hundred-percent honest and from his heart.

Remy had the scene rehearsed in his mind. Through all of his SEAL training, he'd learned that every operation, properly rehearsed, stood a better chance of successful completion. He'd even practiced getting down on one knee, falling sideways several times before he got it right. Maybe practicing was overkill, but he wanted the proposal to be perfect. Mitchell wouldn't have any excuse to refuse his offer of marriage based on his performance.

When he emerged from the bedroom with his suitcase and hers, he set them on the floor and grinned. "Are you ready to go on vacation?"

Mitchell sighed and shook her head. "I have to admit, I had second thoughts."

Already tied in knots over the big step he was taking, Remy's stomach twisted even more. "And?"

"And…" Her lips lifted on the corners, and with them, his spirits. "I'm ready to get away. With you."

"Then let's get to the airport. I hear it's a pain getting through security at this time of day. So the earlier, the better."

The drive to the airport was fairly uneventful, other than rush-hour traffic clogging the roads and the on and off ramps to the bypasses and major roadways. Every time a vehicle pulled up beside theirs, Mitchell studied the windows, looking for sinister faces or the barrel of a gun poking through.

When they finally arrived at the airport parking lot, she was exhausted from the tension and worry of not knowing whether the adjacent car had tinted windows because it was hiding one of Rocco's men, or a baby's car seat.

With over an hour until their flight departed, Mitchell figured they had plenty of time to check in and wade through the long TSA security line.

Remy stepped aside and let her onto the escalator first. "How long has it been since your last vacation?"

Before she could respond, she felt the hairs on the back of her neck prickle and stand on end, and she almost missed her footing as she stepped onto the escalator. "I don't know," she answered, trying to focus on the question while she turned and scanned the faces below. None of them were familiar, or appeared to be anyone other than normal passengers on their way somewhere for the Christmas holidays. "Maybe five years." She gave it more thought. "Make that ten. Must have been my senior trip after high school graduation. I went to Pensacola with friends."

"Babe, you're long overdue." He grinned and winked.

"What about you?"

Remy pointed to the top of the escalator. "Watch your step."

Mitchell turned just in time to step off the escalator. "Well?"

"*I'm* not having a problem concentrating on where I'm going. I know when to get off the escalator." He laughed and slapped her fanny. "Lighten up. You're on vacation."

Mitchell liked that he teased her. His gentle banter eased the tension and made her feel more...feminine and desirable, and less keyed-up over the possibility of being targeted by a psychopath.

Working as an agent, she felt like she had to be as tough as the next guy to fit in with the male majority. She met the men's fitness standards, performing as many pushups and sit ups as her male counterparts, and she ran as fast as most. On the range she was as good as, or better than, most men and women. She fired expert on her Glock, a nine-millimeter Berretta and the Sig Sauer.

The security line moved at a snail's pace. Several large families with small children fumbled with all the paraphernalia associated with traveling with little ones. Backpacks for each, strollers, diaper bags, toys. The only two lines open with scanners were backed up to the escalator.

Toys were dropped, the baby spat his pacifier out. Milk bottles were double-checked, and by the time the children were all run through the body scanner, half were screaming or crying.

Remy grinned the entire time, while Mitchell's stress climbed.

As she emptied her belongings into the bins to be x-rayed, Mitchell reminded herself she was one step closer to leaving Norfolk. One step closer to freedom from worry for the next week.

"See that little girl?" He pointed out a girl of about four, with long, straight, light blond hair. "I can picture you like that at that age."

Mitchell shook her head. "My hair was like that until my mother died. Then Dad kept my hair cut short until I learned to do it myself." She didn't add that her father didn't want to touch her hair. It reminded him too much of her mother's.

Remy smiled at the little girl on the other side of the barrier. "Have you ever thought what having children of your own would be like?"

Mitchell frowned. For so long, she'd only

dreamed of being an NCIS agent, solving crimes, putting away bad guys and moving on to the next case. When she'd agreed to marry Derek, she'd pictured their lives pretty much continuing as usual—the only difference being that she'd come home to a man in her apartment occasionally.

With Remy, he reminded her daily of his family, talking about how his little sister was in college now, and his older brother had just gotten a promotion and had a second kid on the way. Mitchell shrugged. If she was truthful with herself, she'd have to say 'yes.' She'd thought of a little Remy running around the living room like his hair was on fire. Or a miniature, female version of the man, with dark hair and dark eyes, bouncing on Remy's knee and squealing delightedly.

But that was moving their relationship to a place she hadn't wanted to consider. They lived together and shared all their free time. Wasn't that enough? She forced herself to shrug. "I hadn't really thought about it. With both of us working in the fields we're in, doing so isn't practical."

He glanced over his shoulder. "I love my job, but I don't see myself being in the field forever."

Again, Mitchell hadn't thought beyond working cases and undercover ops. Deep down, she was afraid to commit to more than the next day. Her mother's death had left her father devastated. She was afraid of loving someone that completely.

She'd taken a big step agreeing to marry

Derek, thinking that losing someone you loved didn't happen that often. To have someone to come home to could be worth the risk. When he'd come home in a box, she'd been shocked.

Sure, he was a Navy SEAL. Their job was one of the most dangerous in the world.

Remy stepped aside to let her pass through the full body scanner first. She stood with her feet apart and held her hands over her head. The light moved from one side of the machine to the other.

"Step through, ma'am," the TSA agent said. "I'll need you to step aside."

"Why?" she asked, glancing back at Remy as he stood with his hands over his head. The machine beeped, he stepped back out of the scanner, rummaged in his pockets and pulled out what appeared to be a wad of something, maybe a box that had tape wrapped around it. He palmed it, casting a furtive look her way.

"Ma'am, please stand with your feet spread and your arms straight out from your sides."

Mitchell returned her attention to the female TSA agent wielding a wand and complied with her demands, raising her arms to the side.

The agent skimmed the wand over the tops of her arms, under her arms, and down her sides.

With nothing to do but stare at the clock on the wall in front of her, Mitchell noted they only had ten minutes until boarding began. Anxiety twitched her muscles, but she forced her body to remain still. Hopefully, this scan wasn't going to take much longer.

The wand moved down her right leg, up the inside of that leg and down the other one without a single beep, and the agent stepped back.

Mitchell was so confident she was in the clear, she turned to retrieve her shoes and laptop.

"Ma'am, I'm sorry, but you'll have to come with me." One of the agents manning the X-ray machine had joined the female agent and held Mitchell's bag and computer.

"What's wrong?" Mitchell asked. The one holding the bag gave her a narrow-eyed look that made Mitchell's belly flip.

"We need to perform a more thorough search of you and your belongings."

"Have you found something that makes you think I'm a risk? My flight boards in less than ten minutes." She reached for her belongings, but the man held them away from her. "I just want to get out my wallet. I'm an NCIS agent. Surely, there's nothing suspicious about me."

"Ma'am, just follow me." The female agent and the male carrying her bag and laptop surrounded her and herded her toward a side door.

This wasn't right. She was NCIS. A federal agent. Mitchell looked over her shoulder.

Remy cleared the body scanner on his second trip through. When he spotted her being led away, his brows dipped. "What's going on?" Grabbing his things, he hurried after her, still in his socks.

The female agent blocked his path. "Sir, you'll have to wait outside while we search the female passenger."

His brows dipped even lower.

Mitchell gave him a twisted smile. "I'll be out in a minute."

"I don't like it. Have they told you why they're targeting you?"

"No." The door closed between them, and Mitchell crossed her arms. "Why am I being searched more? Is this a random check?"

"No, ma'am." The male pulled her purse out of her backpack and handed it to her. "Please show me your identification."

Her pulse rate jumped. "I showed it to the man at the beginning of the security line. He told me I didn't have to have it out anymore."

"Please comply, ma'am."

Mitchell pulled her driver's license and NCIS credentials out of her purse and handed them to the man.

"We have a police officer on his way here to verify your identity. In the meantime, our personnel will be conducting a more thorough search of your person."

"What?" Mitchell backed up a step as the door opened and another female TSA agent entered. "I'm a federal agent. You have my credentials." She pointed at her identification. "That's my picture on the badge. What more do you need?"

"I'm sorry, but your name came up on our watch list as a person of interest, a potential terrorist."

Mitchell's jaw dropped. What the hell? "And my NCIS badge isn't enough to convince you that I am who I am?"

"Identification can be forged, ma'am. Your best bet is to cooperate until this matter is cleared." The male TSA agent left the room.

Mitchell couldn't believe this was happening. "Call my boss. He can vouch for me."

"Our supervisor is working on it. In the meantime, we're here to perform the search of your person. Please remove your clothing down to your underwear."

Knowing resistance would only make things worse, slow the process, and more than likely make them miss their plane, Mitchell complied, removing her boots, jeans and sweater. "I'd like to know who put me on the watch list in the TSA system," she muttered. "You're going to find this is a big mistake."

"Maybe so, but we'd rather be safe than sorry," one of the female agents said. "We're responsible for the safety of every man, woman and child on board each aircraft."

"No kidding." She fought to keep her voice calm. "Which is why you should be searching for real terrorists, not one of the good guys—me."

The agents examined her clothing in minute detail and ran detection swabs over everything. Finally, they handed back her clothing.

With quick moves, she dressed and then propped her hands on her hips. "So? Am I free to go?"

Both of the women shook their heads.

One went to the door and opened it enough to nod to someone outside. Then she closed it and faced Mitchell. "If you're cleared by our supervisor, you'll be allowed to go."

If, not *when*.

After fifteen minutes confinement in the room, Mitchell was ready to climb the walls and rip a new asshole out of the one responsible for entering her name into the system.

She had her suspicions, but held her tongue until the lead TSA agent entered, and held out her driver's license and NCIS credentials.

"Your identification checked out, and you're free to go, Agent Sanders. Our apologies for keeping you, but I'm sure you understand."

She took the items from him and crammed her purse into her backpack, biting her tongue. If she made too much of a stink, the TSA might mark her as belligerent, and a threat to other passengers.

Remy was outside the door, pacing away from her when she emerged. He spun and raced back in her direction. "What the hell's going on? They wouldn't tell me anything."

"I'll tell you once we're on our flight."

He glanced at his watch. "They might have closed the doors by now."

"They better not have." She grabbed his hand. "Let's go."

They half-walked, half-ran to their gate.

Mitchell was afraid that if they flat-out

sprinted, someone might pull them aside again, maybe at gunpoint, claiming they were suspicious or potential terrorists.

The desk agent at their gate was talking to a last-minute passenger and his wife as Remy and Mitchell arrived.

"Have they closed the door yet?" Remy asked.

"No, sir. Are you booked on this flight?" she asked.

"We are."

"Names, please."

They gave her their names and waited while her fingers flew over the keyboard. Then her eyes narrowed and her lips thinned. "I'm sorry, but we just gave your seats to someone else."

Remy smiled his killer smile at the agent. "Can't you give them back, since we are here?"

"I'm sorry, but it clearly states you have to be at the airport early for your flight."

"And we were. The TSA detained us, or we would have been here in plenty of time."

The attendant's brows furrowed, and she swept her gaze over Mitchell and then Remy, lingering on Remy's broad shoulders.

Already on her last nerve, Mitchell clenched her fists to keep from reaching out and slapping the stupid smile off the woman's face.

"Let me check again." She ran her fingers over the keyboard for what seemed like another ten minutes. "As a matter of fact, we had a couple of cancellations. I can get you both on the airplane, and the next one in Atlanta."

"You canceled that one, too?" Remy asked with an edge to his voice.

"When you didn't make this one, it would have done no good to hold the next one," the attendant stated, as if to a particularly dense child. "But don't worry. I got you on that flight, too."

Mitchell released the hold her teeth had on her tongue and forced a smile at Remy. He'd planned this entire vacation and had seemed so excited about taking her to Colorado. She was glad she didn't have to disappoint him.

The woman handed them two individual boarding passes. "Please board immediately. The flight attendants will be closing the door any minute."

Mitchell snatched the boarding pass, hiked her backpack up on her shoulder, and ran down the sky bridge to the aircraft, with Remy on her heels.

They arrived at the door as the attendant was reaching out to close it.

"Please, take your seats immediately. The plane will be taking off as soon as everyone is seated and buckled in."

Mitchell looked at her pass and hurried down the aisle toward her seat. When she reached it, she realized it was a center seat, and people were in the ones on either side. Disappointment drooping her shoulders, she looked back at Remy. "What seat do you have?"

He glanced at his boarding pass. "Actually,

I'm back a row or two." Remy looked over her shoulder at hers. "This is yours?"

She nodded.

Remy's lips pressed together. "Not what I had in mind."

"Me either." She checked her connecting flight and his. "Looks like we'll be split on the next one, too."

"Great." Remy shook his head.

"At least, we're on the flights."

"There is that." He didn't look happy. "Hey, kid, do you mind switching with me?" Remy asked the boy in the aisle seat.

The boy pulled one earphone from his ear and glanced at Remy's boarding pass. "No, thanks. I prefer the aisle." He plugged his earphone back in and ignored Mitchell and Remy.

"Whatever happened to teaching your kids to respect their elders?" Remy muttered and turned to find his seat.

Mitchell pointed at the seat in the middle. "I'm there."

The teenager sat in the aisle seat, listening to his music, blatantly ignoring her.

She tapped his shoulder, and he glared and pulled his knees in, but didn't get out so that Mitchell could step in easily.

She had to climb over him to reach her seat. Before she could find her seat belt, the flight attendant was there, telling her that as soon as she was buckled in, they could leave.

From where she sat, Mitchell could see

Remy. He was already in his seat, surrounded by two pretty young women, probably in their early twenties, who were laughing and giggling at something he'd said.

Mitchell's hackles rose, and she curled her fingers into the denim of her jeans since the teenager on one side and the bulky man on the other had already claimed the armrests. Sandwiched between the two, she tried to relax, but couldn't.

So far, this vacation had been more of a pain in the ass than fun. She made a mental note to ask Remy to make their next vacation within driving distance.

The plane taxied down the runway and lifted into the air. Even though they were finally on their way, Mitchell's stomach still roiled over being on the TSA watch list, and the hairs on the back of her neck prickled. The feeling that someone was staring a hole into the back of her head made her crane her neck, but she couldn't see over the top of the seat.

She closed her eyes and tried to nap through the flight. Because she knew Rocco was still on the lam, Mitchell chalked up the ultra-awareness to paranoia.

Chapter Five

REMY KEPT up a game face throughout the flight. He had planned on sitting beside Mitchell, holding her hand, letting her know how much he cared. Instead, he was seated between two pretty girls, knowing that wouldn't go over well with Mitchell. She was fully confident in herself as a person. But, she did have a few image issues about her femininity. Although she'd proven she was up for the task when she'd posed as a pole dancer at Rocco's strip club.

Holy shit, she'd been so hot, Remy hadn't recognized her. Just the thought of her in that stripper outfit had his body heating and his member hardening. When the flight attendant came by with the drink cart, he asked for ice water, hoping to chill his libido before he embarrassed himself and scared his seatmates with a huge lump growing in his lap.

So, things hadn't quite turned out the way he'd liked getting through the airport and onto the plane. He'd arranged for the cabin he'd rented to be perfect, having paid extra for the real estate company to provide an iced bottle of champagne and rose petals spread across the king-sized bed. As a last minute addition, he'd called a florist and had them deliver an embarrassingly large bouquet of roses in all shades available—just to make sure he had every meaning for the colors covered. Mitchell meant everything to him, from friendship, to passion, to joy. He couldn't wait until Christmas morning when she opened her gift, and he got down on his knee and proposed. He had it all planned out.

From the first moment he'd met Mitchell, she'd made it clear that she wasn't much of a romantic, but Remy was enough of one for both of them. Though she hadn't spoken much about her childhood or previous relationships, he suspected reticence had to do with her upbringing. She had told him that her father raised her, which would explain a lot.

Remy had been around when she'd been engaged to Derek, before he was killed during an operation. Derek had bought her flowers one time, and though she scolded him because cut flowers died, Remy had caught her burying her face in the blossoms to inhale their scent. She'd been pleased with the gift, even if she wasn't very good at expressing it.

Though he would have preferred sleeping away the hours in flight, the two ladies on either side of him insisted on entertaining him the entire trip. By the time the plane landed at the Atlanta airport, his ears were ringing and he couldn't wait to get on the next plane, with Mitchell beside him.

She only spoke when necessary. They could sit for hours in comfortable silence without feeling the need to break it just for the sake of hearing noise.

Once the sky bridge was pushed up to the plane and the passengers started disembarking, he moved to the side to allow others to pass until Mitchell made her way toward him. Then he stepped into the aisle in front of her. "How was it?" He glanced over his shoulder at his future fiancé. If all went well, in less than three days time she'd be accepting his offer, and they'd celebrate over a bottle of champagne and a soak in the cabin's hot tub, naked.

She shrugged. "Okay. I'm ready to get there. One more flight. After we land in Denver, how long is the drive to where you're taking me?"

He grinned. Other than the flight details, he hadn't told her where in Denver they were going, only to bring clothes to ski in. "About two-and-a-half hours."

"That gets us there around ten o'clock. Will we be able to get into our accommodations?"

"I have all the details worked out. We'll get in."

Using the underground train, they found their way to the next gate.

As they walked through the terminal, Mitchell kept looking around at the moving people, her brows furrowed.

"Something wrong?"

Her lips pressed together briefly before she smiled. "No. It's just a bit crowded."

"All these people are probably trying to get home for the holidays."

"And we're getting away from home." She hooked his arm in hers and leaned against him. "Have I said thanks for making me take a vacation?"

"When you put it like that, trip doesn't sound like fun."

"Oh, but it is. I'm terrible about taking off time." She squeezed his arm. "Thanks."

"Don't thank me yet. We aren't there."

"True. But we're away from Virginia, and the drama there."

They boarded their plane and once again sat in their assigned seats with five rows between them. This time, Remy sat between a business man and an old man.

Mitchell was tucked between a woman with a lapdog barking beneath the seat in front of her, and a very tall man who kept putting his legs out in the aisle.

Not exactly according to Remy's plan, but they were getting there. He even managed to take a short nap on the three-hour flight. The descent into the Denver airport was a bit choppy, but the plane landed safely.

Again, Remy waited for Mitchell on the sky bridge, and they followed the signs to the baggage claim carousels where they waited for bags from their flight.

Within fifteen minutes, the bags had all been loaded onto the carousel. Remy claimed his, but

Mitchell's was nowhere to be seen.

"You're kidding me." Mitchell laughed and shook her head. "I cannot catch a break today."

When the last passenger grabbed his bag, the remaining bags were piled to the side—none of which were Mitchell's.

"My personal handgun was in that bag. I can't just leave and risk it being set aside like these." She waved at the suitcases piled up with no one watching to ensure the right people claimed them.

"Let's go to the lost baggage desk. Maybe they can locate the bag." Remy guided Mitchell to the room labeled Lost Baggage Claim for their airline.

The woman behind the counter had circles beneath her eyes and a red, dripping nose. "How can I help you?" she said in a hoarse voice, and then sneezed into the crook of her arm. "Sorry. I've got this darned head cold, and nothing seems to be kicking it. My nose has been running like a faucet all day."

"My bag didn't arrive with my plane." Mitchell handed her the baggage claim ticket and stepped out of spray range.

The woman pulled a tissue out of a box beside her keyboard and blew her nose before keying the number into the screen. After several minutes of alternating between wiping her nose on the tissue in her hand and racing her fingers across the keyboard, she looked up. "I'm sorry, but your bag was held up at security in Norfolk. It did, however, make it onto a later flight in Atlanta, and will be on the next flight arriving in two hours."

Mitchell looked from the woman to Remy. "Two hours?"

Seeing her slack-jawed amazement, Remy chuckled and cupped her elbow. "That will give us time to get the keys to our rental car, have a leisurely dinner, and for you to have a glass of wine before we get on the road. It'll be okay."

Mitchell allowed Remy to lead her away to find a restaurant. "Two hours means it will be after midnight before we arrive at our destination."

"I know." Remy slid a hand along her back. "Just that much longer to enjoy the anticipation of the surprise."

Mitchell breathed in and let go of a long breath. "I'm not very good with surprises."

"I promise, this surprise will be worth the wait." Remy dropped his bag and rubbed her shoulders, amazed at the amount of tension he could feel in her muscles. "You didn't sleep on the plane, did you?"

"No."

He continued to massage the back of her neck, wishing things had gone much smoother. "Are you afraid of flying?"

She leaned her head forward, giving him better access to rub the muscles in her neck. "Not at all."

"You never got to tell me what went down

with the TSA."

"I will, over dinner. Let's get the keys to our car." She glanced at the stack of unclaimed bags. "I'd say leave my bag, but I can't when it's got my weapon inside."

He bent to retrieve his bag and took Mitchell's hand in his. "We're staying until it arrives."

"What if it doesn't show up on the next plane?" Mitchell argued.

"It will. The clerk wouldn't have known to tell us it was on the next plane from Atlanta if it hadn't shown up on the flight manifest. The bag will be here."

They walked back through the busy airport and found a restaurant. The hostess led them to a quiet table in a corner. They ordered appetizers. Mitchell ordered a chicken salad and Remy ordered a burger and fries. As they lingered over their meal, Mitchell told Remy what had happened in Norfolk.

"I bet that bastard Rocco had something to do with me being added to the TSA watch list," Mitchell said. "I should have shot him while I had the chance. He has access to some talented hackers to get into that system."

"I'm sorry you had to go through the hassle in Norfolk."

"It wasn't your fault. Speaking of being on the TSA watch list, do you mind if I borrow your phone?"

Remy pulled his phone out of his pocket and

handed it to her.

She called her boss in Virginia and told him what had happened. "What's the status on the search for Rocco?" She paused, listening. "Nothing? Damn. You have Remy's number now. Please keep me informed. Yeah, I know I'm on vacation, but I have a stake in this. It's my ass he's after."

Mitchell hung up and handed back Remy's phone, then let out a sigh. "Patrick promised to check into the watch list and see what he could do to fix the hack into the computer system. Hopefully, he'll have me off it before our return flight."

"We need to get you a new phone," Remy said, tucking his into his pocket. Remembering the panic he'd felt during minutes they'd been separated made his gut clench. "I don't like that if I lost you in the airport, I couldn't find you."

"I can pick up a disposable phone. I bet there's a shop here."

They'd managed to spend an hour and a half of their two hours over the meal.

By the time Remy paid the bill, they discovered most of the shops were closed. Fortunately, they did locate a newsstand that also carried gadgets and disposable phones. They purchased one and activated it on the spot.

Remy checked the arriving flights, and spotted the one from Atlanta. Things were looking up. After the delays, they would finally be on the road to their destination where he'd spent a good chunk of his savings to secure the nicest cabin for this special occasion. So they'd had a few setbacks. Their trip could only get better from here, right?

Fortunately, Mitchell's bag was on the carousel, and they were reached their rental car with no further incidents. On the two-and-a-half hour drive along interstate seventy out of Denver, she focused on relaxing. The feeling of being watched had persisted all the way from Norfolk, through the Atlanta International Airport and on the flight to Denver. Every time she turned around, she didn't see anything or anyone that raised alarms. She'd even made trips to the lavatory on both planes, just to see if she recognized any faces she should be concerned about.

The ones she *could* see clearly didn't ring a bell.

Now that she and Remy were alone, she let herself relax and start feeling a little of the excitement he radiated. She glanced out the window, enjoying the sight of snow-covered hills. "Why is everything a secret? Why not tell me where we're going and what your plans are?"

Remy shot her a smile. "I thought a woman liked her man to be a little mysterious."

"What? More advice from your buddies?" She shook her head. "For the record, this woman isn't interested in having her man be a little

74

mysterious"

He winked, stirring up the little butterflies that always fluttered in her belly when he did that. The man didn't have a clue how sexy he was, and what his smiles and winks did to her insides. If she had her way, they'd have stopped at the nearest hotel and started their vacation there, making love through the night. All this traveling was cutting into the time they could be spending together, just the two of them…in bed…naked.

Somewhere between Idaho Springs and when they turned off the interstate highway onto a state highway, Mitchell fell asleep. She woke when the turn signal clicked and the vehicle slowed. "Wh…where are we?" She straightened, tipping her head side to side to work the kinks out.

"Almost there."

"Where is there?" She yawned and stretched.

"Check out the sign." He slowed as they approached a blue sign at the side of the road.

"Vail!" Mitchell leaned forward and her breath caught in her throat. "You're taking me to Vail?"

"That's right."

Her excitement waned. "But isn't that crazy expensive?"

"Not if you get a package deal and lock in three months in advance."

"You've been planning this for three months?" Her heart sank further. Not only had he spent a lot of money on this trip, he'd been planning it for so long. Hell, she hadn't even gotten him a gift or put any thought into the trip. Damn it, the man deserved better than her.

"Why did you bring me, Remy?" Jerking her left leg onto the seat, she turned to face him. "You could have brought a friend who skis a lot better than I do. I've only been on beginner slopes, and only twice during college."

He laughed out loud. "Take a friend? Babe, *you're* my friend. And I don't care if you ever ski. I want to spend the time with you, not someone else. And I definitely don't want to spend time with anyone else naked, like I plan on spending with you."

"Are we staying at one of the resort hotels?"

Grinning, he shook his head. "Nope. Wait until you see the place I have reserved." He drove through the picturesque town of Vail, decorated in twinkle lights and Christmas wreaths. The view was like a photograph on a Christmas card. He passed the huge resorts at the base of the ski slopes and turned onto a narrow road that led up the side of a hill. "Not much farther. Look for the mailbox."

As they rounded a corner, flashing red lights rose above the tree line like spotlights and reflected off the heavy layer of snow coating the trees and hillside.

She scooted forward. "Looks like there might be emergency vehicles ahead. Maybe they're following the snow removal equipment."

"I don't know. That's a lot of red flashing lights."

When he rounded another corner, he nearly ran into the back of an SUV marked Eagle County Sheriff. Ahead of it was another Sheriff's SUV and several Vail city police vehicles. But the sight of two long, red-and-white fire trucks made her catch her breath. Smoke billowed out from a location at the center of the vehicle convergence. "We shouldn't go in there. Looks like they're working a fire."

Remy studied the mailbox on the other side of the sheriff's vehicle, and then glanced ahead. "Damn." He pulled to the side of the road, turned off the engine, and got out.

Mitchell grabbed both of their jackets and hurried after him, glad she'd worn her boots that morning, instead of tennis shoes. Snow and ice crunched under her feet as she slipped her arms into the sleeves of her insulated jacket. The acrid scent of smoke stung her nose and lungs, but she didn't stop until she caught up with Remy.

He headed straight for a cluster of people, one of whom appeared to be in charge, alternating between talking on a radio and to the men working around the towering flames spewing from the hull of what once had been a building. Pushing into the crowd, he spoke to the leader, his brows dipping.

Mitchell caught up with him. "Remy, we really shouldn't get in the way." She laid a hand on Remy's arm and tried to draw him back. "We should go to our rental and leave them to their jobs."

Remy snorted, the warm air pushed from his lungs making steam come out of his nose. "That would be kind of difficult."

Mitchell half-listened as she held his coat out to him, urging him to shove his arms into the sleeves before he got frostbite. "Why would that be difficult? Surely, there's another road around this traffic jam."

"Maybe, but the house fire they are working is the address of our mountain getaway cabin."

Chapter Six

HER HANDS FROZE in the process of helping him drag his jacket up over his shoulders. "What?"

He nodded toward the house. "That burned-out hull was where we were supposed to stay."

Mitchell's heart sank into her boots. "You're kidding, right?"

"Wish I were." He zipped his jacket and slipped an arm around her waist. "I guess this mountain cabin is out of the question. What say you and me go find another place to stay?"

The frigid cold seeped through the opening of her own winter coat, and the wind stung her cheeks. "Maybe we should go back to Virginia. I'm getting a bad vibe about this vacation."

Remy's dark brows dipped as he stared down at her. "Babe, things can only go up from here. I promise to make it better."

She looked up at him. "I think the odds are against us."

"I consider it a challenge."

"You SEALs are far too optimistic."

Remy puffed out his chest. "The only easy day was—"

"—yesterday." She took his hand. "Come on,

let's find a warm room with a soft bed before morning."

Thirty minutes later, and at their fourth large resort complex, Mitchell was beginning to curse the No Easy Day philosophy. Already past midnight, they were starting into their second difficult day in a row.

Remy marched up to the desk with a smile. "Please tell me you have one empty room. If you don't, we will be forced to sleep on one of the couches in your lobby."

Tired and past caring if the young woman behind the counter smiled at Remy and batted her eyes, Mitchell was ready to kiss her, if she found them a room with a bed. Three other resorts with their hundreds of rooms were completely full.

"It's Christmas season, and we're usually sold out by Thanksgiving," the previous three resort clerks had each explained.

This resort was their last chance. If they didn't find a room, they would be forced to head back to Denver. Mitchell was beginning to think that was a great idea.

"As a matter of fact, we had a two-room cancellation earlier this evening, due to weather in Chicago. I've filled one of those rooms, but the other is still available. But it's the honeymoon suite."

"We'll take it." Remy slapped his credit card on the counter.

Mitchell caught his arm. "You might want to ask how much it is. Sounds expensive."

"I don't care. We need a room. It's the only one available." Remy squeezed Mitchell's hand. "Let me worry about it. I haven't been on vacation in years, and I promised you this one would be special." With a wide grin at the clerk, he repeated. "We'll take it."

A sleepy bellman gathered their bags onto a wheeled cart and led the way to the elevator. When the doors opened on the top floor, Mitchell and Remy followed the bellman down the long hallway to the end room.

Remy opened the door with his keycard and held it open for the bellman, who entered, unloaded the cart, and backed it out of the room.

"Thank you." Remy shook hands with the bellman, leaving behind a twenty in the man's palm.

The ever-thrifty Mitchell could appreciate the smile on the bellman's face, but she worried that Remy was being too extravagant. "You don't have to impress me by spending a lot of money." She started across the threshold, but Remy grabbed her arm and pulled her back.

"It's the honeymoon suite. We might not be married, but we should honor the tradition."

Before she could figure out what the hell he was talking about, she was scooped up into his arms and carried across the threshold.

She wrapped an arm around his neck, finding being cranky with the man very difficult. After all, the trip was *his* vacation, and *his* money. He worked hard, was in constant danger, and deserved some downtime between missions, and she was one lucky girl to get to spend it with him.

As the door swung closed behind them, Mitchell kissed his lips, loving the way he kissed back. Everything with Remy was full-on. He never did anything half-assed. Including his kisses. It only took one of those maddening smooches to rock her core and make her so hot she could warm the entire room.

His tongue swept past her teeth and claimed hers. Without breaking the connection, he lowered her legs and let her slide down his front, over the hard ridge beneath his jeans.

Oh, yeah, he was as hot for her as she was for him. They never lacked in that department. And after a very long day, anticipating getting him naked, the time had arrived to make it happen.

Mitchell kissed him hard and pushed him to arms' length. "Let's start this vacation."

He grinned. "What you're trying to tell me is that you're tired, and ready to get some sleep?"

"Right." She shook her head and unzipped her winter jacket, letting it drop to the floor. Stepping away, she backed toward the bedroom of the suite, crossed her arms in front of her, grabbed the hem of her sweater, and yanked it over her head. With another step backward, she unbuttoned her trousers and slid down the zipper, her hand slipping inside to cup her own sex, teasing him with the possibilities. She knew how aroused he got when she pleasured herself.

His eyes widened, his nostrils flared, and he

followed her, one step. His jacket flew across the room. Another step and his shirt followed.

Mitchell toed her boots, kicking them off, almost losing her balance in the process. She dug her hand in her pocket for the condom she'd tucked away that morning and held it up. "Wonder if we'll need this."

"Damn right, we will." Wearing a wide grin, Remy advanced.

Mitchell backed away. When she finally let her trousers slide down over her hips, Remy was almost on her.

Laughing, she turned and ran for the bedroom.

He caught her as she burst through the door.

Swinging her up in his arms, he carried her to the king-sized bed and tossed her onto the mattress.

Mitchell landed across the puffy, white down comforter, wearing nothing but her Christmas-red panties and lace bra. Too busy focusing on his hot look to scan the bedroom furnishings.

Remy stood back, naked and rock hard, his gaze sweeping over her, pausing at the bra before moving lower to the panties. "Nice."

Warmth filled her chest and rose into her cheeks at the gleam in his eyes. Not the typical girly-girl, she was glad she'd taken the time to find the matching undergarments at the local Victoria's Secret store while Remy had been deployed. Not that the satin-and-lace wisps would be on her for long.

He crawled into the bed beside her and lay on his side, his finger tracing the pattern of the lace on her bra. "Are these my Christmas presents?"

The reminder that she hadn't gotten him a gift made her heartbeat slow for a moment. With two days left to shop before Christmas, she had to find time and the privacy to get into a store in Vail and buy him something. Hell, this vacation alone was costing him a lot. The least she could do was find a gift that meant something, that had thought and heart in it. God, she was awful at romance!

Remy slid down the straps of her bra, exposing one full breast. "You're frowning."

"Sorry." Mitchell's breath caught when he pinched the tip of her nipple between his thumb and forefinger.

"Were you thinking about Rocco?" he asked.

She took the easy out. "Some."

"Then I'm not doing my job." He winked and bent to take her nipple into his mouth, tonguing the tip into a tight little bud.

Her insides tightened in anticipation of more. "Better?"

"Mmm." Mitchell arched her back, pressing her breast deeper into his mouth. "Yesss." She reached behind her and unhooked the catch on her bra, eager for him to take the other breast and suck it hard. The attention he gave each had her entire body warming, her blood coursing through her veins, the heat pooling at her core.

"Tell me what you want," he insisted.

He never took her needs for granted. A woman could get used to having him make love to her. "Naked," she whispered.

Remy released her nipple. "What?" He kissed a path down her ribs to her navel.

"Not fair that you're naked, and I'm not." Her voice hitched as his finger pushed aside her panties and slid into her.

"We can fix that, you know." He chuckled, the warmth of his breath heating the little triangle of fabric covering her sex, causing her nerves to ignite and her channel to moisten.

"By all means." She hooked a thumb in the elastic band of her thong panties and slipped it down over her hip.

Remy took charge of the elastic band at the other hip, tugged it downward and off her legs, dragging his knuckles over her skin.

The rough texture of his knuckles scraping across her skin sent shivers of desire through her body. When she finally lay naked against the comforter, she let her knees fall to the side, opening herself to him.

He settled between her legs and kissed the tuft of hair at the apex of her thighs. "Is your day getting better?" Parting her folds, Remy blew a gentle stream of air over her heated flesh.

"Oh, yes." She dug her fingers into his thick, dark hair and rode the waves of lust building at her center, radiating outward.

With a stroke of his finger across the

sensitive strip of nerves, he had her body tense, her breathing compromised. He replaced his finger with his tongue and laved her in a long, sweeping stroke, sending her rocketing toward the heavens. Her body pulsed with her release, the sensations so potent they stretched on, sending tingling bursts of electricity to the very tips of her fingers and toes. Finally, she sank back to Earth.

After a last caress of her hip, he climbed up between her legs and claimed her lips once again, his mouth tasting of her musk. He reached for the condom she'd laid on the pillow beside her, tore it open, and rolled it down over his engorged member. Then he paused with his cock poised at her entrance.

Mitchell grasped his ass and tried to pull him into her, but he withheld.

"Mitchell Sanders, you are an amazing woman."

"You're not so bad yourself, frogman," she said, her voice raspy, her satisfaction incomplete, dependent upon him filling the aching, throbbing empty space between her legs. "Please," she begged.

"I will. But first, I wanted to tell you how much you mean to me."

"You've already told me."

He shook his head, a patient smile on his face. "I want you to know that what I feel for you isn't just about the sex." Tipping his head to the side, he grinned. "Although that's great."

Her patience thinning, she wrapped her legs

Wrapping her hands around his neck, she pulled down his face, praying the chemistry they had between them was enough to make him want to stay with her, or at least come back after each deployment. "Make love to me before I forget what it feels like."

Remy thrust into her, his cock surrounded by her heated moisture. Her channel contracted around him, drawing him deeper until his balls slammed against her bottom. God, she felt so damn good, he could die now and have known absolute joy.

He settled into a rhythm, pumping in and out of her, the movement so natural, the sensations incredible.

Mitchell wrapped her legs around him, digging her heels into his buttocks, urging him to thrust harder, deeper and faster. He worked it, his muscles tensing, the nerves throughout his body on sensory overload as he struggled to prolong the ecstasy as long as possible before he catapulted over the edge. The pressure built with every stroke, the friction sensitizing him in the most primal way.

When he couldn't hold back any longer, he thrust deep and held.

Her legs tightened, locking him in.

For a long time he pulsed inside her, relishing every second, feeling more complete than ever before in his life. This woman was the ying to his yang, the Bonny to his Clyde. Oh, hell, she was the only woman for him, and he wanted to make their relationship official sooner than later. He wasn't entirely certain he could wait all the way until Christmas to ask her to marry him, even though he'd been planning this for the past three months.

With all the bad luck they'd had lately, the perfect time might never happen.

When at last he lay down beside her, he rolled her onto her side, to maintain their connection. "Yeah, you're a keeper," he said.

"If only for the sex," she finished.

"Nope. I only need you. I could actually go an entire minute or two without sex, believe it or not." He winked and kissed her forehead, her eyelids, and the tip of her nose, finally settling his lips over hers.

"Yeah, yeah," she said when he eventually let her breathe again. "You might be able to wait a full minute or two, but I couldn't. I don't suppose you're ready to go again?" She trailed a hand over his naked hip and grasped his butt cheek, pressing him closer.

Still hard, he could feel the magic beginning all over again. "Always ready with you, babe. Always." He stripped the old condom and applied a new one.

This time she pushed him onto his back and kissed him, taking control of their lovemaking.

He liked that about her. She could give as good as she got. She straddled his hips and settled herself over him, taking him all the way inside.

Then she lifted up on her knees and slid back down, her long hair moving in waves. "Like that?"

Hardening inside her, he moaned and half-closed his eyes. "You know it, babe."

Mitchell lifted his hands from her thighs and placed them over her breasts, rocking up and down, faster and faster.

He squeezed her breasts, pinched the nipples, and then left them to grab her bottom and lift her up and down faster.

When he came, she did too, her back arching, a low moan rising from her throat. After the tension released from both of their bodies, Remy guided Mitchell back to the bed and into his arms.

"This vacation is getting better by the minute." Mitchell yawned and stretched her body, beautiful in the light from the nightstand. Within minutes, her eyelids drooped and her breathing grew slower and more even.

Remy lay for a long time, staring at her, drinking in the vision of her lying against the sheets, her long, sandy-blond hair splayed out in a fan across the cream-colored pillowcase.

Sticky from traveling, he rose from the bed and hurried to the bathroom for a quick rinse in the shower. He didn't want to be away from her any longer than he had to. Every minute with her was precious. In just two short days, he'd ask her to be his wife. He sure as hell hoped she'd say 'yes.' If she said 'no,' the refusal might ruin what they had at that moment. The risk was one he was willing to take.

Chapter Seven

AN INCESSANT RINGING pierced the cocoon of Mitchell's sleep, forcing her out of the warmth and comfort into the cool room. She lay naked against the sheets, the chill of the night washing over her as she felt for the warm, hard body that should be next to her. "Remy, could you answer the phone?"

He didn't respond, and his side of the bed was empty. As her senses kicked in and her brain connected with her hearing, she made out the sound of the shower behind the bathroom door and smiled. Remy wasn't far. Rolling to her side, she reached for the phone that hadn't stopped ringing. "Hello?"

Silence.

A shiver shook her body, and she grabbed the sheet and blanket, pulling them up over her body. "Hello," she said again, anger rising at the rude call in the middle of the night. Again, no response. She leaned over to hang up the phone when a voice caught her attention, and she froze.

"For every action, there is a reaction. Yours is coming."

Dread settled in her belly like a lead bowling ball. "Who the hell is this?"

A soft click sounded, and the line went dead.

Anger pushed past dread, rising like a tide. Mitchell yanked the phone over close to her and dialed the operator.

"What can I do to help you?" asked the operator.

Most likely the night clerk. "Can you tell me where the last call to my room came from?"

"No, ma'am, I can't. Although it was an outside call. Why?"

"No reason. Thank you." She hung up the phone and sat upright in the bed, chewing on her fingernail. Couldn't be Rocco. He wouldn't be stupid enough to follow her all the way out to Colorado. He would have had to fly, to be here as quickly as she was.

Which would explain the feeling of being watched at the airport in Norfolk and Atlanta. But he wasn't stupid enough to get on the same plane as she'd flown on, was he? She closed her eyes and waded through her mental images of all the passengers on the two planes. Another thought struck her. Rocco might not have been on that plane, but one of his henchmen could have been, and she wouldn't recognize his face. He could be anyone.

Mitchell's gut clenched.

"What's wrong?" Remy stood in the doorway to the bathroom, a waft of steam surrounding him and making its way into the bedroom. His body was covered in a damp sheen of moisture and he had a towel draped around his neck, his dark hair black and wet.

"Wrong?" Mitchell's pulse raced. The man was beyond sexy, and she couldn't believe he wanted to be with her.

"Your face was white, and you looked like you'd seen a ghost." He strode across the room and sat on the edge of the bed. "Are you okay? Was the trip too much for you?"

"Seriously." Mitchell laughed. "I'm not that big a wimp. It's just that the phone rang again."

"Did you answer?" His gaze pinned hers.

With a nod, Mitchell glanced at the phone on the night stand.

"Who was it?"

"I don't know." A shiver rippled across her body.

Remy wrapped an arm around her and pulled her against his warm, damp chest. "What did he say?"

"'For every action, there is a reaction. Yours is coming.'" She connected with his gaze. "You don't think Rocco followed us here, do you?"

"I don't see how he could, unless he came by private plane. Every law enforcement organization in Virginia is hunting him."

"In Virginia," Mitchell said softly with a head shake. "But not in Colorado. Where's that disposable phone?"

"On the desk."

Mitchell threw back the blanket and hopped out of the bed, padding over to the desk. The cool mountain air made her skin pebble and her nipples tighten. The phone lay where she'd left it. She picked it up and dialed her boss's personal cell phone number.

"You realize it's only five in the morning back in Virginia."

"Patrick is usually up by four." She waited for the ring tone.

On the fourth ring, he picked up. "Yeah."

"Patrick, it's Sanders."

"Sanders. You get a new phone?"

"Yes, I did, after my other one was compromised by Rocco."

"What happened? Did he get to this one too?"

"No. Maybe worse." She drew in a deep breath. "I got a call at the hotel room where we're staying in Vail. I think it was Rocco."

"You're in Vail?" Patrick chuckled. "That frogman is pulling out all the stops, isn't he?"

Mitchell glanced at her SEAL, her heart warming. "Yes, but what worries me is how Rocco knew where to find me, because we didn't know we'd be staying here until we got to town and found our cabin had burned to the ground."

"What?" Patrick exclaimed.

Mitchell pushed a hand through her hair. "Yeah. We were two hours late getting here, only to find that a fire gutted our rental cabin."

"Coincidence?" Patrick prompted.

"I thought so at first," Mitchell responded, forcing her shoulders to relax, "but now I'm second-guessing that conclusion."

Remy leaned close to her other ear and whispered, "No such thing as coincidence."

She'd had the same feeling as soon as she'd heard the voice on the phone. "I'd hoped you'd tell me that they caught Rocco, and all this is just one of his minions playing mind games with me."

"Sorry, Sanders. Nothing would give me greater pleasure than to tell you we'd caught Rocco. But I can't. He's still loose, and either he's following you, or he's got someone else on your tail. Do me a favor and lay low. Don't give him any opportunities to get to you. I'll contact the regional office for that area and have them send in backup."

Her thoughts flashed to other agents and holiday time. Mitchell chewed on her bottom lip. "I hate to tie up resources if I'm wrong."

"And I'd hate to lose a good agent if you're not. The federal government put a lot of money and training into you. I can't replace you that easily."

Mitchell snorted. "Nice to know it's all about the money."

Patrick laughed. "Sanders, we love you, you know that."

"I know." Her stance softened and she tightened her grip. Patrick had always been fair with her, and had forgiven her for taking her search for a dear friend onto her own time. If she hadn't, her friend might have been yet another of Rocco's lost or destroyed victims in the human trafficking business. "Say hello to Rita, and give the kids a hug for me."

"Stay safe. I'd hate to have to bring you home from Colorado in a body bag."

"Again, thanks for caring, and the really harsh visual." She hung up and laid the phone on the desk. Tension attacked her muscles and she hated feeling vulnerable. "Rocco's still loose."

"Which doesn't answer the question of how he got here, unless he hired a private plane to make the trip."

"Which he could have done and arrived sooner than us, since we had a layover and were delayed at baggage claim." Mitchell opened her suitcase and extracted her gun case. Flipping the catches, she removed the Glock and loaded it.

"You gonna sleep with that?" Remy asked, his brows rising.

Mitchell grinned at him. "Make you nervous?"

"A little."

"I'm an expert shot."

"I trust you when you're awake, but I'd prefer if you left it on the night stand when you sleep with me."

"Before I moved in with you, I slept with it under my pillow."

"Interesting." He slipped his arm around her waist, plucked the gun from her hand, and laid it on the desk. "Humor me, and leave it on the nightstand. I wouldn't want it to go off accidentally while we were making love."

"That would be hard to explain to the

paramedics, wouldn't it?" Mitchell leaned her naked body against his and absorbed his warmth. "I'll keep it on the nightstand."

"Thank you." Remy kissed her. Capturing her butt cheeks in his big palms, he lifted her and wrapped her legs around his waist. "Let's get some sleep. Tomorrow, we can decide what to do about the phone calls."

Mitchell leaned her cheek against his, liking the way his scruffy beard scraped her skin. "How can I sleep, knowing Rocco might be here?"

"I'll stay awake while you sleep."

"And when will you sleep?"

"While you're awake, holding that gun." He winked and laid her on the bed, dropping down over her. "Now, go to sleep before I think of better things to do." Remy kissed her on the mouth and started to roll off her onto his side.

Before he got too far, she caught him and pulled him back over her, liking how warm and safe he made her feel. "Couldn't we just do those better things and sleep later?"

"Hmm. I might be persuaded." He nibbled her earlobe and trailed a line of kisses and nips down the length of her neck. "Yeah, I could be persuaded."

An hour later, Remy stared at the ceiling with Mitchell nestled in his arms, sound asleep. He'd been slower and gentler as he made love to her the last time, savoring everything about her body and trying to soothe away her fears by giving assurances he'd be there for her and run interference should anyone attack.

Other than having made love to Mitchell three times that evening, nothing else had gone quite the way he'd planned. They had both been so busy in their lives, with missions and training, that they needed this downtime to relax and spend time getting to know each other even better. He'd wanted to woo her and treat her like a princess, letting her know how much he cared, and how their life would be if they were married. In effect, he wanted to give her an idea of what forever together could be like before he popped the question.

Based on the way things were going, forever would be a bit rocky and full of unpleasant surprises, and that wasn't the way he'd planned this trip.

In the morning, he'd see what he could do to find out who else might have checked into the hotel without a reservation, and if they had any connection to Rocco. Perhaps Mitchell could flash her badge and get in to review the hotel security cameras to see if anyone had come through before or after their check-in that might appear suspicious.

With a plan in mind, Remy waited until daylight crept into the window before he allowed his eyes to close and sleep to claim him. With a busy cleaning staff that started early in the morning, he was certain whoever had made the phone calls wouldn't attempt anything stupid with witnesses around.

"Hey, sleepyhead." Mitchell's hand on his shoulder woke him at noon.

She wore a loose T-shirt and flannel pajama bottoms. Her breasts swung free beneath the cotton, tempting the saint right out of Remy.

"I figured you'd want to get some lunch while the resort restaurant was serving, or I'd have let you sleep longer." She brushed a hand across his cheek and waved a cup of coffee beneath his nose. "And I made coffee, just the way you like it."

Remy sat up in the bed, set her coffee on the nightstand and pulled her across his lap. "I'd rather have you."

"Yeah, same here." She nuzzled his neck, and her stomach rumbled loudly. "Okay, so I'm a little hungry, too, which is part of the reason I woke you."

Remy rolled her onto her back and came up on his arms over her. "Who needs food when we can lie in bed all day and feast on each other?"

Remy's stomach rumbled, and Mitchell laughed. "I guess that answers it. Let's go find some food, then we can figure out how we can enjoy this wonderful vacation—given the constraints of a possible vindictive bastard trying to get to me."

"Hmmm. Room service is sounding better by the minute." Remy captured one of her nipples between his teeth through the cotton of her shirt.

"A distinct possibility." Mitchell lifted her shirt to give him better access to the nipple.

He rolled it between his teeth and then pulled it into his mouth, tapping the bud with the tip of his tongue.

Mitchell's stomach rumbled again.

Remy sucked the nipple into his mouth and let go. "As good as you taste, we need to get some food in both of us." He rolled off the bed and stood. "Come on. We can lay around waiting for something to happen, or get out there and make it happen."

Mitchell rolled her eyes. "In other words, we can stay where it's safe, or go outside and make targets of ourselves."

Remy yanked her to her feet. "If you feel more comfortable holing up in the room, I'm all for it. After we get something to eat." He slipped into a pair of sweat pants and marched to the window, sweeping aside the curtains.

Sunshine poured into the room and the mountain rose up before them, blindingly white and steep. The lifts were busy ferrying holiday skiers to the top. Skiers traversed the hill in front of them, some making long zigzags, taking a path from one side of the slope to the other. More daring and expert skiers made tight turns, leaving behind squiggly lines of S's, their knees together, their hips swaying, graceful and effortless all the way to the bottom where they'd again board the lift.

Remy had grown up in Louisiana, but had always wanted to learn to snow ski. It wasn't until he requested cold-weather training in Alaska that he'd first put on a pair of skis. After a few spectacular spills, he'd figured the sport out enough to stay upright. Something about the swishing of the skis on the crusty snow and the pristine white slopes gave him a sense of peace at the same time as it challenged him. He loved skiing.

Mitchell stood beside him. "The view's beautiful."

"I love my home in Louisiana, but the Rocky Mountains leave me in awe." He stared out at the beauty before him.

"I know what you mean." She hooked his arm in hers and leaned her cheek against his bicep. "I used to come here on spring break when I was in college."

"Is that when you learned to ski?"

"Yes."

"Your family never took you on a ski vacation?"

She shook her head. "Dad never even considered it. I didn't know what it was all about until my college roommate asked me if I wanted to come along. I worked as many hours as I could get as a waitress, earning tip money and blisters so that I could go."

"Do you like skiing?"

"I love it," she said, her gaze on the slope in front of them. "It's challenging, and somehow peaceful at the same time."

Remy's heart swelled. This woman was meant for him. They had so much in common it was almost scary.

"What are we waiting for? Let's get breakfast and go rent some skis." Mitchell released her hold and spun away.

"No." Remy caught her hand and pulled her back into his arms. "If Rocco is out there, he'll try something."

"I'm not hiding in our room when there is snow and sunshine out there. I won't be terrorized by anyone. It would be like being held hostage." Her body trembled. "I will not be held hostage again without a fight. Not by Rocco. Not by anyone."

"I almost feel sorry for Rocco if he tries to take you again." Remy smoothed a strand of hair behind her ear. Not the most beautiful woman in the world, Mitchell was strikingly attractive when she was passionate and fierce about something. From rescuing a friend to taking down a bastard who preyed on innocent women, she was a force to be reckoned with.

"Are you with me, or do I have to ski by myself?" She brushed her lips across his.

"Looks like we'll be skiing together."

"Good. Now let's get dressed and get breakfast...or lunch." Mitchell dressed in record time, pulling her hair back into a ponytail.

Makeup-free, her skin was smooth, and her face was pleasantly girl-next-door.

Remy slipped the ring box into his pocket, not wanting to leave it in the room for the maid to find and mistake the tape-covered box for trash. He really needed to stop by a jewelry store and get a new box. He couldn't give it to her like it was. Everything had to be perfect for when he proposed to Mitchell.

If Rocco really was in Vail, Remy's plans could be shot all to hell. When it came right down to it, he didn't mind his plans being ruined as long as Mitchell dodged all the bullets.

Chapter Eight

DRESSED AND READY to go, Mitchell stood by the door, waiting for Remy to pull on his boots. When he straightened, the disposable phone rang.

For a second, Mitchell hesitated answering. After the phone threats she'd received, she'd rather walk around in ignorant bliss than hear another. Then she remembered she'd given the number to her boss. "Hello," she answered.

"Agent Sanders?"

"That's me. Who's calling?"

"Agent Ron Billings from the Denver Field Office. I hear you might need backup in Vail."

Mitchell smiled. Trust her boss to get right on it. "I don't want to call anyone in at Christmas time. I know they'd rather be spending time with family."

"Your boss tells us you have an escapee gunning for you. We'd rather err on the side of caution."

"I appreciate that."

"I'm sending out Agent Thomas Thurmon today. He'll be there in two hours. He's been briefed, and he has photos of Rocco, you, and Chief Petty Officer LaDue. He'll be working undercover as a tourist. I won't have him make contact, unless you specifically need him to."

"Good. I'd rather not let Rocco think I'm running scared."

Agent Billings gave her Thurmon's phone number and his. "If you need any more assistance, please don't hesitate to call either of us. We're the on-call for the holiday."

"Lucky you." Despite what she'd verbalized, she really was grateful for the backup. Mitchell ended the call and saved the numbers in the phone's contact list. "Help is on the way."

"I'm glad to hear it." He took her phone and held it while he tapped on his own. "I'd like those numbers as well. In case you lose or destroy your phone."

His crooked grin made her smile. Mitchell clapped her hands together, feeling a little better knowing they wouldn't be alone. "Let's get this vacation underway with a hearty meal."

They ate lunch in the resort restaurant, and then made their way to the rental shop where they spent the next hour being fitted for skis, boots, poles, and helmets. By the time they were completely outfitted, the time was past two in the afternoon.

"The ski lifts stay open until four-thirty. Purchasing a lift ticket this late in the day isn't worth the cost," Mitchell said, hoping Remy wouldn't be too disappointed. "However, if you want to go for two hours, it's up to you. I'm game for anything."

"I figured we'd hang out at the resort, maybe take advantage of the heated pool and hot tub, and then have a nice dinner in the village."

"Sounds good to me. I'd like to duck into a few shops while we're in the village. I need a new pair of gloves that aren't neon green, and a set of hand warmers for when we are on the slopes tomorrow." Plus, she had yet to get that present she so desperately wanted for him.

"Let's store this gear in the lockers and hit the pool. I could use a workout."

With a plan in mind, they stored their skis and went up to their room to change into swimsuits.

In the elevator, Remy hit the button for the lobby level. "I want to check with the front desk and make sure we're okay for the duration of our stay in Vail."

"Sounds good," Mitchell said. "While we're at it, let's see if they'll let us look over the security video. If Rocco's people are following me, they might be here."

"Good idea."

At the desk, Mitchell flashed her NCIS credentials and asked to see the names of the people who'd checked in the night before, up to four hours before they'd taken the last room. She claimed to be on a surveillance case. No use telling the clerk a killer might be in the area when Mitchell wasn't sure of anything, at that point. She hoped her Denver Field Office counterpart didn't flash his badge here, as well. Two feds seemingly operating separately would draw too much attention.

None of the names the hotel clerk showed her rang a bell or looked out of the ordinary. A couple by the name of Woolsey had taken the second to the last room right before Mitchell and Remy arrived.

"Could we see the security video from last night?" Mitchell asked.

The clerk didn't argue, showing her and Remy to the room where a security guard in a resort uniform monitored twelve screens, alternating between different views of the resort elevators, entryway, and individual floors.

"Let's look at the entrance between eight p.m. and midnight," Mitchell directed.

The security guard brought up a screen to the earliest time and fast-forwarded the video at a pace that would allow them to see who was coming and going. A clump of young people crowded the lobby, carrying backpacks, suitcases and pillows.

"That's the school group from England," the guard commented.

A variety of men and women moved through the lobby. Some carrying skis, others toting suitcases. When they got to the hour before Mitchell and Remy's arrival, a couple was seen checking in at the desk.

"The Woolseys?" Mitchell guessed.

Remy nodded. "Perhaps."

The couple turned so that Mitchell and Remy

could get a good look at their faces.

"Not a threat," Mitchell muttered. The couple was smiling, and appeared to be in their late sixties or early seventies. They rolled large suitcases behind them and looked like any couple coming to a resort to ski, not kill.

None of the people that had come through the lobby looked sinister or suspicious.

With no more useful information than they'd started with, Mitchell and Remy thanked the guard and headed for the pool.

"I feel like I'm being paranoid." Mitchell paused at the door leading to the outdoor heated pool and stared at the steam rising off the water. Snowflakes drifted through the air, landing on the heated concrete deck and immediately melting.

"With someone like Rocco threatening you, it pays to be a little paranoid."

"Yeah, but I don't want him to spoil our vacation."

"Excuse me, miss." A young teenager with pale skin and a shock of red hair squeezed past her and Remy.

Mitchell stepped to the side and a flood of teens raced past, laughing and jostling each other in their hurry to get to the hot tub.

With a smile, Mitchell took Remy's hand. "Come on, let's get in that workout. Maybe by the time we've finished our laps, the hot tub will be empty."

Mitchell hung her towel on a hook near the door and stepped outside. The winter breeze immediately stole her breath away. "Remind me to wear a one piece instead of a bikini."

"The water will feel good."

"It had better." She shot him a teasing grin. "Last one in has to rub the other's back later." Mitchell sprinted for the pool and dove into the water, welcoming its warmth.

Remy dove in beside her, and they matched strokes for the first couple of laps. Though a good swimmer, Mitchell couldn't keep up with Remy. Soon, she slowed, turned over on her back, and let him power on. The man was a machine. A beautiful, sexy hunk of a machine with lovely muscles rippling through the water. He was every girl's dream boyfriend, and Mitchell knew how lucky she was that he wanted to be with her.

Mitchell transitioned into a breaststroke and completed another lap down and back, and came to a stop, letting her feet touch the bottom in water up to her neck to keep the bite of the wind from chilling her too quickly. A lace of ice formed in her damp hair, but she didn't mind. Pausing gave her time to think and ogle the man she loved.

Other than her undercover operation as a pole dancer to blow a hole in Rocco's human trafficking ring, she'd never relied on others to bail her out of a tight situation. Yeah, she was lucky to have Remy. He'd made sure she came out of that action alive. Since then, they'd been tight. Really tight. So tight they'd agreed to live together. But lately, she'd sensed a restlessness in

Remy. Ever since he'd gotten back, he'd been antsy, like he couldn't wait for something more than just a vacation. Some men got restless when they were tired of a situation and wanted to move on.

Mitchell hoped that wasn't the case with Remy. She prayed they could hold it together for a very long time. Wanting more probably wasn't fair when neither of them was willing to give up the jobs they loved. And she wasn't even certain what she meant by "more." Perhaps *she* was the one who was antsy and ready for a change. The one thing she knew for sure was that she wasn't ready to move on.

Remy was so much a part of her life, even when he wasn't there. Everywhere she went, everything she did or saw reminded her in some way of him. Often she caught herself thinking that he would like this, or he would say that. Too often, she worried what they had wouldn't be enough for her or him and, because of their jobs, they couldn't be more to each other.

She would never ask Remy to stop being a SEAL, and he wouldn't ask her to stop being an NCIS agent. That's why she'd never considered the 'M' word. Marriage was for people who had time to spend together. Those people came home at night after a long day's work and watched television together, or argued over the remote control.

Mitchell and Remy were happy when they were in the same country, and ecstatic when they were in the same building. They'd go months without seeing each other, unless Remy had a rare opportunity to talk to her on an internet video call from some hell hole in the Middle East or wherever his team happened to be sent.

The man of her thoughts surged out of the water in front of her, lifted her high, and tossed her in the air. She splashed down, went under and surfaced, laughing. "Not fair. I wasn't ready."

"You were looking far too serious. I had to break that train of thought." He spread his arms wide. "What better way than to dunk you?"

"Two can play that game." Mitchell ducked beneath the surface and made a grab for his leg.

Remy planted a hand on her head and held her away until she had to surface for breath.

"Don't think you're going all caveman on me. I'll get you soon enough. You have to sleep sometime."

"Go ahead. Try me." He raised his hands in surrender, an ornery grin spreading across his face.

Mitchell's eyes narrowed. "You know I can't be mad at you for long." She eased toward him and wrapped her arms around his waist, pressing her cheek to his chest. "Especially when you're all sexy and wet."

"It's that Cajun charm. I'm chock-full of it."

With a snort, Mitchell glanced up at him, her brows rising. "Charm? Not so much. Full of it? Absolutely." She hooked her leg around his calf and shoved hard on his chest, pushing him backward into the water.

He went under, but before Mitchell could congratulate herself on the sneak attack, he gripped her arms and took her with him.

With a quick breath, she went under and twisted her body against his, wishing they had the pool to themselves, instead of sharing it with the half-dozen teens that had spilled over from the hot tub.

Floating beneath the surface, Remy captured Mitchell's face in his hands and kissed her.

She twined her legs around his, and they drifted to the bottom of the pool. Seconds later, Remy pushed them to the surface and held her close. If she could have frozen that moment in time, she would have. She'd never felt more secure and cherished as she did standing in the warm water, the frigid air turning her hair to ice.

A wicked wind blew gritty snow against her skin, causing Mitchell to shiver.

Remy bent his knees, urging her to sink low in the water. "Duck down out of the wind, babe. Can't have you turning into a popsicle."

Mitchell bent her knees, submerging everything but her head. That sensation of something besides snow crawled across her skin. The same feeling she'd gotten on the airplane, and in the Atlanta airport, made her body tense. She glanced toward the building, straining to see into the shadows beneath the eaves. Either someone was watching them, or the paranoia had returned with a vengeance. A pause in the shouts and chatter from the teens gave her too much time to imagine the worst, when nothing had happened but a phone call that could have been placed from halfway across the country.

But how could Rocco have known their cabin had burned, and they had been forced to find this particular alternate lodging for the night?

"You're frowning again." Remy captured her cheeks between his palms. "I'm starting to get a complex."

Glad for the subject change, she swatted at his arm. "That'll be the day. You're so damned cocksure, the only complex you'd have is a hang-up on yourself."

He laid his hand across his heart, his expression serious. "You wound me, Sanders."

"Why don't I believe that?" She patted his cheek and winked.

"You know me too well." Remy grinned.

"Damn right, I do." And she hoped no other woman would ever know him as well.

He caught her hand beneath the water and raised it to his lips. "Ready for that hot tub?"

"You bet." She got out of the pool and let the icy air chill her body for a moment.

Remy climbed the steps and stood beside her. "Feels good."

"For about two-and-a-half seconds." A bone-shaking shiver shook her frame. "I'm getting in." She glanced at the hot tub full of teens splashing water at each other. "Or should we head back to the room?"

"Hit the tub. I might go find a vending machine and get us some bottled water."

"That would be great."

"Will you be okay while I'm gone?"

"I'm a big girl. I can take care of myself." She glanced at the pool teeming with young people. "And I'll have plenty of company."

Remy's eyes narrowed.

Mitchell laughed and touched his arm. "You don't think *they're* out to get me, do you?"

"No," he said.

His expression didn't display confidence at that answer. "Look, babe, I know what Rocco looks like. If I see him, I'll go the other way and notify the police."

Remy laid his hand over hers. "Yeah, but you don't know if he's sent someone else to do his dirty work."

"I'll trust my instincts. I'm usually a pretty good judge of body language." Mitchell stared again at the hot tub full of a dozen teenaged boys, glad they were there, if for nothing but the company while Remy was gone for a few minutes. "I'll be fine."

Remy hesitated a moment longer, and then sighed. "I'll be right back with water."

He waited until Mitchell slid into the steaming tub before he headed into the building.

No sooner had Remy disappeared than a woman poked her head out the door. "Are all of you eating dinner tonight? If so, you have fifteen minutes to shower and dress."

Like a plug had been pulled, the hot tub drained of teens, leaving Mitchell completely alone for the first time that day. She craned her neck to see into the glass door of the building, feeling more than a little exposed.

A cloud chose that moment to obliterate the setting sun and the rays that had teased her into thinking the air was warmer than the actual twenty-five-degree temperature with an even lower wind chill factor.

Then a couple emerged from the building.

Mitchell recognized them as the Woolseys from the video. They appeared to be a nice older couple helping each out over the cold ground to the hot tub.

The woman smiled. "Do you mind if we join you?"

"Not at all." Mitchell moved away from the steps, allowing them easy access into the small pool.

As they settled into the steaming, bubbly water, the door opened again.

Mitchell glanced toward it, hoping to see Remy, but was disappointed when a big man emerged, wearing a pair of cargo shorts, instead of a swimsuit, and carrying a towel.

He glanced toward the pool for a second and then crossed the heated concrete to the hot tub, slipping in, still holding the towel in his hand, above the water.

A tingling awareness rippled across Mitchell's skin, like being overly sensitive to the feathery soft brush of a spider web against her hair. She considered getting out of the tub and going into the building in search of Remy.

"Have you been in Vail long?" Mrs. Woolsey smiled.

The polite question forced Mitchell to engage in conversation she really had no desire to conduct. "Got in late last night," Mitchell said, her words clipped.

"Oh, really? So did we." She glanced at her husband. "George doesn't like to make reservations in advance. We came out from Denver after he got off work, hoping we'd find a cancellation. We went to two other places before we found a room." Shaking her head, she laughed. "I thought we'd have to sleep in the car, or drive all the way back to Denver."

"Glad you found a room," Mitchell said politely.

"Me, too. The clerk said it was one of the last two available." She smiled at her husband. "I'm just glad we didn't have to sleep in the car, right, George?"

"Right, dear."

Mitchell pretended to be engaged in the Woolsey conversation, while she kept watch through her peripheral vision on the man who carried the towel so carefully. He laid it on the edge of the big hot tub and leaned back, his gaze landing on her and narrowing.

He had heavy, dark brows, and brown-black eyes, a thick five-o'clock shadow across his chin, and a barrel chest like a defensive lineman on a football team. A python tattoo wrapped around one of his massive biceps in black and red ink.

Mitchell wouldn't consider him handsome, with his bar-bouncer scowl and thin lips. She'd feel a lot better when Remy returned. If he wasn't back in another minute, she was heading to the room where she'd left her gun. It was kind of hard to hide a Glock in her bikini, or she'd have brought it with her. The man with the tattoo reached for his towel, and Mitchell noticed it had a lump the size of a pistol between its folds.

The man didn't grab for the towel, he slipped his hand between the folds, instead.

Her heart thumping against her chest, Mitchell surged out of the water.

"Leaving so soon?" Mrs. Woolsey asked.

"I think I left the iron on in my room." Mitchell scrambled out of the water and up the stairs, her back to the man. She had to get out of range before the man opened fire. If she didn't, she risked him shooting her and any witnesses, including the Woolseys. Her heart in her throat, her back stiff, anticipating a bullet hitting her square between her shoulder blades, Mitchell bolted for the door.

As she reached for the handle, she spotted Remy stepping through, carrying two bottles of water in one hand. "Mitchell? Are you okay?"

She chopped her hand in the air. "Go back in the building."

He pushed her behind him and stood into

the doorway peering out. "What's wrong?"

"Just come inside," she said in an insistent whisper, dragging at his arm.

Remy backed through, and closed the door. Inside, he set the plastic bottles on a table and gripped Mitchell's arms. "What's going on?"

She shook free from his hold and eased back to the window looking out over the hot tub. "I think that man with the tattoos in the hot tub might be packing." She squinted through the glass, keeping as much out of sight of the hot tub as she could.

Remy pulled her back and placed his body in front of hers. "Why do you think that?"

"There's something under that towel. He was reaching for it when I got out of the pool."

"He's reaching for it now," Remy said, poised for action. "And...it...looks...like a book."

"Seriously?" Mitchell leaned closer to the glass and squinted.

Just as Remy said, the man had pulled a book out of the towel and held it above the bubbling water.

The tension eased from her neck, and she breathed for the first time in minutes. "Thank God."

Remy settled his hands on her shoulders. "Babe, you're all knotted up. Let's go back to the room and relax."

"Do you mind? The Woolseys probably think I'm a complete nutcase. I lit out of there like my ass was on fire."

Remy laughed out loud. "You did look like you were scalded, even though your face was pale." He held out a towel and wrapped her in it. "Come on. Let's go get cleaned up so I can take you out for a nice dinner with a big bottle of wine."

"Thank you for being so understanding." She gripped the edges of the towel under her chin, feeling like a rookie agent. "I much prefer it when my enemy is where I can see him. Then I can just shoot him and be done with it."

Remy patted her ass, sending her lurching forward. "That's my girl."

Though he played it off lightly, Remy was on alert as much as Mitchell. Every time they came to a corner, he edged her back and went first.

Mitchell's heart swelled. She'd never had a man so concerned about her well-being. Though she prided herself on her independence, she enjoyed being spoiled. Hopefully, all the extra precautions were overkill, and her boss would call the next day to let her know they'd caught Rocco. Then all would be right with the world.

Chapter Nine

REMY HAD CHECKED the vending on the floor with the pool only to find sodas. No water. He'd gone to the first floor to the resort shop, only to find the same situation, and the water bottles had been cleaned out. He'd gone up two flights of stairs before he'd found a machine with water bottles. By then, he'd gotten more and more concerned about leaving Mitchell in the hot tub without protection.

On his way back down the stairs, he'd been convinced she was in trouble and he'd raced, nearly breaking his neck on the last flight of steps. When he'd seen Mitchell running toward him, he'd been ready to take on any threat, even throw himself in front of a bullet.

Back in the room, he pulled his H&K .40 caliber handgun from the bag he'd checked onto the plane. As a SEAL, he had access to every kind of weapon he could imagine or ask for. When off-duty stateside, he usually didn't carry a gun, unless he was headed into an area that warranted self-protection. Though he wouldn't normally consider a ski resort a place he'd need to carry his handgun, he'd brought it along, anyway. After

Rocco's threat and how spooked Mitchell was, he trusted his instincts and packed what he might need.

Back in the room, Mitchell hit the shower first.

Remy gave her a few minutes on her own, and then joined her.

She stood beneath the spray, rinsing the shampoo suds from her hair, water coursing down her body.

Damn, she was beautiful. He hadn't gotten into the shower with the idea of making love, but one look and his cock was as hard as steel and ready.

Mitchell opened her eyes, her brows rising up her forehead. "Are you just standing there, or are you making love to me?" She reached out and curled her fingers around his staff, tugging gently.

Remy closed the distance between them. "I didn't bring protection."

Mitchell grinned and reached behind the shampoo bottle. "You mean one of these?" She held out a foil packet. "A good NCIS agent comes prepared."

He took it, ripped it open, and slid it down over his already throbbing member. "You're a woman after my heart, you know that?"

"I know."

Her tone held a sassy confidence that turned him on almost as much as her incredibly toned and gorgeous body.

"Now, do you know what to do with it, or do

I have to take care of that, too?"

Moving with lightning swiftness, he scooped her up by her thighs, wrapped her legs around his waist, and pressed her against the tile wall. "What about foreplay?"

"Overrated."

"I want you to be ready." He rested his forehead against hers.

"Babe, I was ready when I stepped into our room."

He eased into her. "Mmm. Yes, you are."

"Told ya." She smiled and lowered herself over him, taking him all the way inside. "Now show me what you've got, frogman."

Balancing her against the wall, he thrust into her and pulled out, his hands on her hips, guiding the movement, setting the pace.

Mitchell rested her hands on his shoulders and rode him, her head tipped back, her breasts bobbing in his face.

He paused to capture the tip of one perky nipple in a quick nip, and then let go when the sensations ignited inside and sent him rocketing toward the heavens. One more thrust and he tipped over the edge, exploding in an earth-rocking orgasm he wouldn't have expected, standing in a shower for only a few minutes with the most amazing woman in the entire world. "Sorry, that was way too fast," he whispered into her neck, kissing her earlobe.

She dug her nails into his shoulders and moaned. "Baby, don't stop now, I'm almost there." Tightening her legs around him and pushing down on his shoulders, she slid up and down.

Remy threw himself back into the rhythm, pumping hard and fast, sliding his hand between them to part her folds and flick the sliver of flesh he knew would set her world on fire.

He touched her there and she stiffened, her back arching, her mouth open on a silent moan, then she squeezed his shoulders so tightly, he was sure she left indentations, as she rode her own wave of release all the way to the shuddering end.

Mitchell sagged against him and let out a long, satisfied breath. "That was phenomenal."

"My thoughts exactly." Remy eased her off his semi-erect shaft and set her on her feet. The water had gone from steaming hot to lukewarm and getting colder. "We'd better get out before we run out of hot water."

He swept her up in his arms and stepped out of the shower, setting her on the bath mat. Then with extreme care, he dried every inch of her body, taking his time to kiss every surface he touched. Next, she did the same for him, pausing at his cock, smoothing the towel, then her bare hands over its length.

"At this rate, we won't get to the restaurant." Remy gathered her in his arms and pressed his body against hers.

"Who needs food, anyway?" she said.

"I could hold you like this forever," he said into her ear. "What do you say? Are you ready for it?" Though he'd tossed idea out there casually, he held his breath, her answer meaning so much more to him than he could ever have imagined.

"Mmm. I'm ready," she said. "I could eat a sixteen-ounce rib eye all by myself." She sucked his bottom lip into her mouth and let it go. "Let's get going before all the restaurants roll up the sidewalks." With a quick squeeze of his buttocks, she stepped into the bedroom.

Remy let go of the breath he'd held, a little disappointed Mitchell hadn't caught the full meaning of his words. He'd asked her if she was ready for forever with him. Instead, she'd taken the questions as ready for dinner.

He figured it was just as well. That statement wasn't the proposal he had planned so carefully. Until he did it right, it didn't count. Christmas morning, when she opened the little box and found the ring inside, he'd get down on his knees and ask her to marry him. If asking her wasn't enough, he'd beg her to be a part of his life forever. He loved her so much he couldn't imagine living without her.

Dressed in warm slacks, thick down-filled jackets, and insulated snow boots, they stepped out into the winter night.

"Do you want to walk or drive?" he asked.

"We're so close, I'd rather walk."

Walking along the sidewalk that had been cleared of the snow and ice, Remy remained alert for any threat. With the Christmas decorations on every building and bright twinkle lights strung along the eaves, the place appeared to be a fairytale village more than a high-dollar resort.

The restaurant was four blocks from the hotel, with lots of shops and other eateries between. Remy made note of a jewelry shop with extended hours for the holidays that would still be open when they left the restaurant.

The streets and sidewalks were busy with holiday shoppers and tourists, dressed in bright jackets and scarfs, laughing and smiling. Some sang Christmas carols, others window-shopped or strolled hand in hand.

With so many people milling about, Remy was glad when they reached the relative safety of the restaurant and went inside. Because he'd made reservations earlier that day, they were seated quickly. The meal was excellent, the wine took the edge off Mitchell's nerves, and Remy enjoyed himself immensely. When their plates were cleared and he waited for the bill, Remy reached across the table and took her hand in his, his heart as full as his stomach. "I feel like this is our first real date in a long time."

"I know. We seem to see each other only when we're coming and going." She laced her fingers through his and sighed. "Sometimes, I wonder what it's like to be normal people, with normal jobs, who come home every day at six and have dinner by seven and go to bed by ten."

Remy's chest tightened. He couldn't promise her that kind of life. All he could promise was that when they were together, they would love like there was no tomorrow. He'd do his best to make her happy in every way he could.

When they were together. "Is that what you want?" he asked. "The normal life?"

She shrugged. "Seeing each other more often would be nice."

His chest tightened even more. He couldn't give her a normal life. Not now. He could only give her what was normal for them.

Mitchell squeezed his hand. "No. I don't want that kind of life. Not yet. I like what I do. I feel like I'm contributing to the greater good. I like that *you* like what you do. I think you're pretty damned amazing, and I love you for all that you sacrifice for your country."

"You're pretty amazing, too. And you sacrifice no less for justice."

"And while we're physically and mentally able to perform the jobs we've chosen, I wouldn't have it any other way."

"Even if it means we don't see each other very often?"

"We'll make up for lost time." She grinned. "It will make when we *are* together that much more exciting."

"What about when I'm too broken-down to be a SEAL? Will you trade me in?"

Mitchell laughed. "Are you kidding? What man will put up with me and my less-than-perfect attempts at being feminine and romantic?" She tilted her head to the side. "Are you concerned? You? A SEAL with so much swagger you fill every room?" She leaned closer. "Babe, you've got this all backwards. You're the hunk, the badass SEAL. I wear a black trouser suit. What's sexy about that?"

"Sometimes I don't think you realize just how sexy you are, Mitchell." He made sure to infuse his voice with emotion.

"And what's up with my parents naming me Mitchell?"

"What most folks don't see is what *I* see beneath the tough-as-nails NCIS agent. You're the sexiest, most feminine woman around. When you let in someone." Remy stared into her eyes, as if he could see the future in her gaze. But he couldn't. Christmas morning seemed such a long way away, when in fact it was a day and a wake up.

"Yeah, well, I'm not always so good at letting in people. Now am I?"

"Then I count myself as extremely lucky." The waitress left the bill on the table. He dropped a hundred dollar bill on it and stood. "Ready to go back to the hotel?"

"As long as we get to stop at a couple of the stores on the way."

Remy pulled her to her feet and kissed the tip of her nose. "That can be arranged."

The walk back along the sidewalk was no less crowded, with even more people out than earlier.

"I want to duck in here." Mitchell stopped in front of a leather shop next door to the jewelry store Remy had wanted to stop at for a new ring box.

"Okay," Remy said, his gaze intense. "Stay inside until I come back to get you. I'll be in the shop next door."

"Deal." She opened the door, and the smell of new leather wafted out.

If he didn't have a mission of his own, he'd have gone in with her. The smell of fresh leather reminded him of wallets, knife scabbards, and saddles. Growing up in Louisiana, he'd had friends who kept horses. He'd mucked stalls for the opportunity to ride. He wouldn't mind perusing the leather store, but first, he had to get the box he needed.

After a thorough glance around at the people near the shops, searching for anyone who looked like he might cause problems, Remy entered the jewelry store.

Men liked leather, didn't they? Didn't matter what the item was as long as it was leather and had that great leathery smell, right? Mitchell went through the entire store twice. A knife sheath was too warlike. Remy didn't have a horse, so a saddle or saddlebag wasn't practical. A wallet seemed overdone, even if he'd keep it with him almost always, and she didn't want to get him a black leather jacket without him trying it on for size. Though, wearing a black leather jacket would make him look even more badass than he already did.

A whip was too Indiana Jones, a cat-o-nine tails was… Hmm, she lifted the item and slapped the strap end against her open palm. Shivers rippled through her body. He'd spanked her before and the act had been an incredible turn-on. But gifting him the cat-o-nine tails gave him more control.

She trusted him, but was she willing to give him that much power over her? To do so would be to give up some of her control. Since the beginning of their relationship, she'd stressed her need to be independent, to be the master of her own destiny. Mitchell had never wanted to rely on anyone but herself for her happiness. All the years wishing her father could show her half the love he'd felt for her mother had broken her of that. She created her own happiness.

How soon that changed after she fell in love with Remy. For a SEAL who killed for a living, he was the kindest, most gentle man she'd ever known. Even when he'd spanked her, he'd been considerate enough to ask her if it hurt and lightened his strokes accordingly. Mitchell couldn't imagine living without him in her life. Part time or full time.

On more than one occasion, she'd told Remy she wanted to keep things just the way they were, and not take the next step most people made in their relationships. She'd claimed their jobs as the obstacle keeping them from moving forward. But plenty of women had Navy husbands who were gone nine months out of the year. Even more

Army wives whose husbands deployed for fourteen months.

If she was honest with herself, she was afraid to give her heart completely. If Remy died in a particularly awful battle, she'd be heartbroken. That thought made her throat tighten. Hell, she'd already given him all of her heart, wittingly or unwittingly. And now that she'd told him she wasn't interested in changing things from the way they were, she wanted more.

She'd have to find a way to tell him how much he meant to her, and that she wanted him in her life on a permanent basis. Well, as permanent as their crazy schedules would allow. She wanted him to be hers, and vice versa.

She stared around at the leather in the shop. "Now what gift says all that?"

None of them. Still, she purchased the cat-o-nine tails, because she liked the smell and the way it felt in her palm. But she wasn't satisfied with only that.

The clerk had just bagged her item when the bell over the shop door rang.

Remy entered, scanned the room, and then met her gaze. "About done shopping?" he asked.

"I'm done shopping here. But I'd like to go to the jewelry store for a few minutes." She waved around the room. "Why don't we switch? They have some amazing knife scabbards over there against the wall." She hoped he'd go for it. She'd need a good chunk of time to find the perfect gift in the jewelry store.

"Great. I love the smell of leather." He carried a small bag displaying the name of the jewelry store.

Damn, had he bought her another gift? Mitchell's stomach knotted around the rib eye steak she'd eaten. She had to make a decision quickly. Christmas was only a day and a half away.

Remy walked her out of leather shop and into the jewelry store, kissing her on the lips before leaving her alone with the gemologists.

As soon she watched him leave, she turned to the woman behind the counter. "I want a gift for the man who just left that isn't too girly and that will tell him how much I love him without being too gooey."

The woman narrowed her eyes and touched a finger to her chin. "How about a pocket watch?"

Mitchell thought about her suggestion, but wasn't sure the watch was Remy, or made the statement that she wanted to convey. "What else do you have?"

"A thick chain necklace in silver or white gold."

"No. I can't imagine him wearing a necklace other than his dog tags." Mitchell spun around, staring at the glass cases of diamonds, colored gemstones, earrings and rings, and she wrung her hands, losing hope of finding him anything that spoke of her love and how much she wanted to be with him.

"How about a ring?" the clerk suggested.

Mitchell stopped in front of a case of men's

rings. "A ring." The thought took root and grew. She faced a case with thick silver and white gold bands. A dark gray one shone up at her with a chip of a diamond embedded in the metal. It was sleek and masculine. "What about this one?"

"That's made of titanium. The metal is amazingly strong and is very difficult to destroy. It should last forever."

"Forever." Mitchell slapped her credit card on the counter. "I'll take it. Could you wrap it for Christmas and hide it in a big bag so he can't guess what's inside?"

The woman nodded, grinning. "Gotcha. One big bag coming up."

Moments later, Remy entered the store, thankfully after the clerk had taken Mitchell's purchase to the back room to wrap and bag.

"Ready?"

"Almost." Mitchell couldn't believe how excited and nervous she was about the gift she'd chosen. Christmas couldn't get there fast enough. And yet, the day would come far too soon.

The clerk handed her a large bag stuffed with tissue paper, and the light weight indicated it also contained the small box with the ring inside.

Mitchell hooked it over her arm, thanked the clerk, and headed for the door.

"What did you find that you couldn't live without?"

She almost answered *You*. Instead, she bit down on her tongue in time, phrasing her response in such a way she wasn't fibbing. "Not tellin'. But, I did find something I couldn't live without."

"Really? And you're not going to share it with me?"

"Nope. Not yet." Butterflies fluttered in her belly at the thought of giving Remy the ring. Would he think she was asking him to marry her? Her knees shook at the thought, and those butterflies turned into condors, flapping their wings against the inside lining of her gut. Holy hell. Mitchell almost spun on her heels and returned the ring.

Yes, she wanted to be with him forever, but Remy was just as much a free spirit as she was, and might not want to be tied down. No, this was wrong. She turned to go back into the store, her feet cold from years of experience.

The clerk clicked the lock and flipped the open sign to Closed. Wiggling her fingers at Mitchell, she smiled, spun, and walked to the rear of the building, turning out the lights as she went.

"Did you forget something?"

"My mind," Mitchell muttered, then straightened her shoulders and faced the man she couldn't imagine life without. "Let's go to the hotel."

"Did you find a new pair of gloves?"

"No. I decided I could live with neon green. If I drop one in the snow, I'll always be able to find it."

"True." Remy scratched his chin. "Hmm. What item could you purchase that you couldn't live without?"

Mitchell smiled, but didn't offer an answer. *Let him guess.*

A crowd of young people pushed past them on the sidewalk. One of them wore a dark jacket with a hood.

When she realized he would run right into her, Mitchell stepped back.

Remy pulled her into the protective circle of his arms and blocked her body with his.

The hooded man slammed into Remy, knocking both of them back against the building.

"Hey!" Remy shouted and shoved away the man.

The crowd of young people moved on. The man in the hooded jacket split off from them and ducked down an alley.

"Are you all right?" Remy steadied Mitchell and frowned. "Those kids need to be more careful."

"No kidding. Look what they did to your jacket." Mitchell pulled on the sleeve.

Remy glanced down at his arm. The feathers in his goose down jacket were flying all over the place from a nine-inch rip in his sleeve. His gut clenched. "What the hell?"

Mitchell studied the tear closer. "Looks like someone ripped your jacket on purpose. With a knife."

Remy spun, looking for the guy in the hooded jacket. He was nowhere to be seen. He'd been aiming for Mitchell when Remy cut in front of him. If he'd gotten to her, he might have succeeded in tearing more than her jacket. Anger and fear burst through him. Anger that anyone would make a stab at Mitchell. Fear that he'd almost reached her. "Come on." Gripping her arm, he guided her along the sidewalk. Anytime someone got close, he angled his way in front of Mitchell, using his big body to shield hers.

"Remy, stop." Mitchell ground her feet into the sidewalk and pulled him to a halt.

He tried to drag her along, but she refused to cooperate. "We need to get back to the hotel."

"That knife was meant for me, wasn't it?" she demanded.

Remy thought about lying to keep from worrying her, but knew she'd see right through him. "Probably."

"If he'd really wanted to kill me, do you think he would have been so clumsy?"

"I don't know. What I do know is that I don't want you hurt."

Mitchell raised a finger. "On the trip here, I felt like someone was watching me at the airport in Virginia, on the planes, and in Atlanta. Call it paranoia, call it intuition. I don't care."

"Why didn't you tell me?"

"I didn't see anyone who looked suspicious. Why worry you?"

"Because I'm there for you." He tightened his grip. "Damn it, Mitchell. You can trust me."

"I know. This vacation means a lot to you, and I didn't want to mess it up if my funny feeling was unfounded." When he started to say something, she held up her hand. "Then when we got to Vail, the cabin we were supposed to stay in was burned to the ground." Her brows rose. "I know it wasn't a coincidence."

"Then the call, and now the attempted stabbing."

"Whoever is doing this is playing with me."

Remy's lips pressed together in a tight line. "Rocco wants you scared."

"Yeah, but when does he go from scare tactics to kill tactics?"

"Never, if I can help it."

"Did you happen to see the guy's face? The one who stabbed your jacket?"

Remy shook his head. "No. The hooded jacket shadowed his face just enough to keep me from identifying him."

"Okay, something's definitely going on, but we don't know what the game is, and who Rocco has put behind it."

"Should we head back to Virginia?" Remy would leave immediately if Mitchell wanted him to.

Mitchell shook her head. "What good would that do but put us closer to more of Rocco's people? At least here, there shouldn't be that many of them. We could draw them out."

Remy blinked, his belly clenching. "You mean lure them...as in baiting a trap."

Mitchell nodded. "Yes."

"No." He didn't like where the conversation

was heading. "I can't believe you think you'll be the bait."

Mitchell raised her hands, palms up. "They are trying to get to me. Let's give them what they want."

Before she finished her sentence, Remy shook his head, dread weighing him down. "No. That's insane."

"Let's go back to our room and discuss this. We need to come up with a plan."

"We'll go back, but we're not planning anything that sets you up as bait. Think about what happened last time you let yourself be kidnapped. You were nearly sold into the human sex trade."

Mitchell planted her hands on her hips, her chin rising. "And I'm still here to talk about it. Everything turned out okay in the end." Her arms dropped to her sides. "Except that Rocco got away and is now out to kill me. But I can—"

"I know. You can take care of yourself." He hooked her arm and dragged her along with him. "Come on, Ms. Independent, let's go back to the hotel."

"Right, let's head back to the hotel so that we can come up with a plan to reveal our attackers."

Remy chuckled. "You don't give up easily, do you?"

"Not when it's important." She leaned into his side. "This vacation is as important to me as it is to you. I'm tired of letting someone else run the show. Let's turn the tables on them."

Chapter Ten

MITCHELL SAT BESIDE Remy the next day on the Born Free Ski Lift, headed for the top of the mountain, her thoughts on the knifing of the night before and what might occur on the slopes that day. Why couldn't they have a normal vacation?

When they'd returned to their hotel room the night before, she'd been surprised by a bouquet of roses in every imaginable color. The arrangement had been lovely and filled the room with its heavenly scent. Remy admitted he'd ordered them for the cabin, and had the florist deliver them to their room instead.

He'd been a gentle and attentive lover, taking his time to bring her to an orgasm before perfecting the night with one of his own. Afterward, they lay for a long time, basking in the afterglow of incredibly hot sex, talking about the future and the possibility of one day living in Colorado, preferably in the mountains.

For some couples, the more time they spent together, the more faults they found in the other. Not with Mitchell and Remy. At least on Mitchell's part. Every day she spent with Remy only made her want to spend another together.

He was perfect. She couldn't find one thing wrong with him.

She sighed as she faced the challenges ahead and the mountain slope in front of her, her legs dangling from the chair of the ski lift. This plan had to work, or their vacation was doomed.

"I'm still not happy about this idea," Remy repeated for the fifth time. "Your boss said that if you needed help, you should call him or the regional NCIS office. I'd say this is a good time to call for backup. We should make contact with Agent Thurmon."

"We don't know how many people we're dealing with. If it's just the one guy from last night, we can take care of him ourselves."

"If it's an entire platoon of Rocco's men?"

She smiled. "Then we're screwed, and you can tell me I told you so."

"I'd rather be wrong in this case," he grumbled, shifting his ski poles so that he could pat his ski jacket.

Mitchell patted her pocket, searching for the hard outline of her handgun. "Look, if it gets sticky, we'll call in for more backup."

That they were both armed did a little toward reassuring Mitchell. At least, they could defend themselves, if they had to. With her Glock inside her jacket pocket, she wouldn't be a complete sitting duck. The ski slopes were her idea. If Rocco's man was that determined to follow her, he might come out to the slopes to knock her off. What better place to ditch a body?

And having them out on the slopes gave her and Remy a better chance of spotting them first, than running into them on a dark street or in a stairwell. Not to mention, fewer people would be hurt if bullets started flying. "We don't even know if Rocco's men can ski. This could turn out to be a perfect vacation day of well-maintained ski runs and sunshine." She patted his leg. "Stop worrying."

"Then stick with me. Promise me you won't go hot-dogging down the slopes. I'm not even sure I remember how to ski."

Yeah, right. "Like I've had much more practice than you? You got the intensive cold-weather training. Not me. My skiing consisted of several winter and spring break visits to the slopes in New Hampshire, not the Rockies. There are real mountains here with steep slopes."

"Guess we're about to find out how good we are." He lifted the bar over their laps, and they both scooted to the edge of the seat, preparing to dismount the lift.

"The first time off the lift is the hardest. I'm always afraid I'll disgrace myself and crash and burn."

"Focus, Sanders. You've got this." The lift chair slowed at the drop-off point. Remy leaned forward and slid down the icy ramp onto hard-packed snow.

Mitchell wobbled, then found her ski legs and glided toward Remy, turning her skis in a sharp sideways motion to stop, kicking up the snow in front of her. "Feels good, doesn't it?"

"Yes, it does." Remy grinned and pulled down his goggles over his eyes.

Settling her goggles over her eyes and wrapping the pole straps around her wrists, Mitchell gripped the handles and dug them into the snow. "Green, blue, or black?"

"Let's start with green and move up to blue on the next run."

"Good." Mitchell brushed her neon green glove over her forehead. "I was afraid you'd start with something with more of a challenge, and I'd fall so hard, I'd have a yard sale first day, first run."

Remy's eyes narrowed. "Yard sale?"

Mitchell laughed. "When you hit so hard that everything you're wearing is scattered across the snow like a yard sale."

"No yard sales today. Come on. Let's get our legs under us, and watch out for anyone on our tails. And since you're the one they're targeting, you get to go first so I can keep an eye on you."

"Bossy, are we?" She dug her ski poles into the crusty snow and slid toward the signs indicating which slopes were green, blue, and black. Choosing a long, easy green, she started down the wide open slope, practicing her turns until her hips and knees felt natural. Several times, she glanced over her shoulder.

Remy kept pace, his movements smooth and effortless, his feet tight together, both skis moving as one, forming tight S's in the groomed snow.

They enjoyed the day skiing, despite having to keep vigilant about the other people on the slopes. Lunch was at a restaurant at the top of the mountain, where they sat outside in the sunshine, eating a hearty vegetable soup in a bread bowl. When they finished, they lingered a little longer before getting back out on the slopes.

After lunch, they graduated to the intermediate blue slopes and made several passes along the more challenging runs. They'd agreed not to try the black slopes. If Rocco's men followed them up the mountain, they'd want to be on a course that didn't require complete concentration like the ultra-steep grades and moguls of the black diamonds.

Mitchell hadn't skied enough black runs to consider herself an expert skier. Blue was enough to satisfy her desire for a challenge, and Remy easily kept pace.

On their last run of the day, the sky clouded and snow began to fall. By the time they got off the lift at the top of the mountain, the wind had picked up, blowing a gritty snow sideways, making it feel as though they were being sandblasted.

"Last run?" Remy asked.

Mitchell nodded. "I'm ready for the hot tub."

"Let's do it." He nodded for her to lead off.

As she skied the hill, she glanced back on occasion. The snowfall was thickening, getting close to blizzard force. At one turn, she looked back.

A snowboarder was flying down the hill,

jumping the slight bumps in the trail and barreling down the slope like a bulldozer. He turned to catch another hump in the snow close to where Remy was.

Mitchell yelled a warning, but the wind whipped away the sound.

The snowboarder flew over the top, landed hard and skidded sideways, plowing into Remy, knocking him over.

Already committed to the turn she was in, Mitchell couldn't slow fast enough to keep in sight of Remy and to see if he was okay. When she could stop safely, she walked sideways up the hill on her skis, one painful step at a time, backtracking to the bend in the trail so that she could check on Remy.

The roar of a snowmobile engine made her think of the mountain rescue team. Had Remy been hurt so badly someone had sent for them? How could they have been notified so soon, unless someone with a radio had happened upon him? Her heart hammering against her chest, Mitchell tried to go faster in her effort to sidestep up the hill. Just when she'd reached maximum frustration level and had stopped, preparing to kick off her skis to walk the rest of the way, a snowmobile roared around the bend and raced toward her.

Mitchell raised her hands and waved at them, hoping they'd slow and let her know whether or not the basket on the back contained the man she couldn't imagine living without.

The driver pulled up beside her.

"Did you just pick up a man who was knocked down by that snowboarder?" she asked, having to shout over the wail of the wind now blowing so hard, she could barely see twenty feet.

The driver didn't answer, but revved the engine. The passenger straddling the seat behind him jumped off the vehicle and ran toward her.

At that moment the fact registered they weren't wearing the red and black jackets of the ski patrol, and that there wasn't a big white cross on the back.

Instinct kicked in. Mountain rescuers would have responded to her question and wouldn't be running straight at her. Too late to unzip her pocket and reach for her gun, Mitchell dug the tips of her poles into the snow and pushed off.

The man hurtling toward her threw his body at her, only capturing one of her ski poles.

Because the strap was wrapped around her wrist, he swung her around before she could shake him loose. Regaining her balance, she pushed her poles into the snow and shoved off, taking the steepest slope to gain speed as quickly as she could. The snowmobile would easily catch up to her.

Her best bet was to duck into the trees, but that was almost as dangerous as trying to outrun the men on the snowmobile. Her skills skiing weren't that good. Sticking to the open slope as long as possible, she skied as fast as she could, the wind blowing against her, impeding her progress.

The roar of the snowmobile engine echoed off the trees, getting louder the closer the vehicle came. Mitchell aimed for a gap in the trees, praying she could get there before the snowmobile reached her.

As she shot toward the relative safety of the tree line, she caught her ski on a crusty lump of snow and she flipped over, tumbling down the hill. Her boots broke loose from the ski bindings, her head hit the packed snow so hard, her helmet could only do so much.

A gray fog moved in on her peripheral vision, dimming the white snow blasting sideways.

No. She couldn't pass out. Mitchell tried to fight back the encroaching darkness only to lose out to the inevitable, consumed by oblivion.

Remy lay on his back, fighting to catch his breath. The snowboarder had hit him so hard, he'd been knocked flat on his back, the air forced from his lungs with a whoosh. As he lay still, struggling to breathe, a snowmobile roared past him, a basket on the back draped with a bright red waterproof tarp. When he tried to sit up, he was knocked down again, this time on purpose. What the hell?

The snowboarder grabbed one of Remy's ski poles from where it had fallen and hit him in the chest.

Before he could roll over, he was crushed by the other man who landed on top of him and smashed the pole against his throat. His breath cut off, Remy thrashed in the deep snow, grasping the pole in an effort to ease it off his throat. Once he had enough air in his lungs, he bucked and rolled to the side, throwing off his attacker.

The heavy ski boots weighing him down, Remy lunged toward the man who'd knocked him off his skis, realizing it had all been planned. If they out took Remy, they could get to Mitchell. The longer he fought the snowboarder, the more time they had to find and capture, or kill, her.

Adrenaline surged through Remy as he landed on top of the man and jerked the hat from his head. He didn't recognize him, and he really didn't care. Yanking off his glove with his teeth, he slugged the man in the face again and again until he laid still, blood seeping from his nose and a cut on his cheek, his body limp.

Remy climbed to his feet, a sharp pain piercing his chest. Probably a broken rib. Nothing that would kill him, which was more than he could say about Mitchell. He gathered his skis and poles, snapped his boots into the bindings, and unzipped the pocket holding his gun.

With only a quick glance at the attacker, he pushed off, stabbing the snow with his poles to build up speed fast. The snow was coming down like gritty grains of sand, hitting hard against his goggles and limiting his visibility to only twenty feet ahead. He followed the tracks of the snowmobile around a bend in the trail, praying he'd find Mitchell waiting patiently.

The trail was deserted, the only indication anyone had been there was the tracks of the snowmobile, quickly being filled by the steadily falling snow. Remy raced down the slope, pushing hard with the poles and bending low to limit wind resistance. Still no Mitchell, and no snowmobile. At several points, he could swear he saw the thin tracks of skis beside the wider snowmobile tracks.

His heart thundering against his ribs, he flew down the mountain. The tracks led toward a stand of trees, swerved, and seemed to slide to the side at the edge of the forest.

Remy slowed to study the tree line, praying Mitchell had made it into the forest where a snowmobile would have difficulty zigzagging through the trees. He almost missed the bright, neon green glove half-buried in the snow, a ski pole lying with only the webbed tip sticking out nearby. His heart slipped into his belly as he dug the glove out of the snow and held it to his cheek. There was no doubt in his mind that whoever had been on the snowmobile now had Mitchell.

Shoving the glove in his pocket, he hardened his resolve and pushed off, racing down the slope, following the tracks, hoping they wouldn't disappear before he found Mitchell. At a trail crossing, the tracks turned off onto a maintenance road that cut across the mountainside.

The snow had thickened, and now came down so hard Remy could barely see the tracks. If he didn't catch up soon, he wouldn't find her. With the storm descending with force over the mountain, daylight was cut off and the dark gray of a winter's night settled around him.

Pulse racing, Remy pushed on. Failure was not an option. He refused to come down off the mountain unless the snowmobile left first.

Darkness and the blinding snow threatened to obliterate his view, and when the road angled upward, Remy slowed on his skis. No amount of poling would get him up the increasingly steep grade.

He stopped, removed his skis, slung them over his shoulder, and trudged uphill, staying between the stands of trees that were nothing more than a darker shadow on either side of the road in the ever-increasing gloom.

By now the slopes were empty, all other skiers having headed down the mountain before the storm got too dangerous. The grooming tractors wouldn't start work until the early hours of the morning, after the snow stopped falling. Groomers worked through Christmas and all holidays when there was snow on the mountain.

Climbing the hill, his heavy boots sinking into two feet of snow with each step, he couldn't help thinking he was moving too slow. Every minute Mitchell was out of his sight was one more minute Rocco's men could use to hurt her.

At the top of a rise, he paused, catching his breath while studying the ground in minimal lighting. He dug his smart phone out of his pocket and used the flashlight app to get his bearings and determine the direction of the snowmobile tracks. He remembered he'd entered the NCIS agent's number in his contact list and dialed. Shoving the phone under his helmet, he cupped his hand over the mic and his mouth so that he could be heard over the howl of the wind.

The agent answered on the first ring. "Hello."

"Agent Thurmon, Remy LaDue. Agent Sanders has been taken."

"Where are you?"

"On the mountain. Someone on a snowmobile snatched her from the slope."

"Damn," the agent said. "Look, the storm is predicted to get worse. You need to come down from the mountain now."

With the cold wind biting his cheeks, Remy tightened his grip. "I can't. She's still up here, as far as I can tell. I need you to find out if there are any cabins or maintenance sheds south of Eagle's Nest Ridge? If I'm having trouble seeing through this storm, they will have had to stop as well."

"I'll get with the mountain patrol, and also have a snow crawler sent your way. I retract what I told you before. No use trying to get down the mountain now. It's too dark and dangerous. We'll come to you."

For the short time he'd been standing still, Remy's body temperature had dropped, and his toes were numb with cold. Sliding up his neck scarf over his chin, he slipped his boots into the ski bindings and pushed off. The road went downhill at a slight descent, giving him just enough momentum to climb the next rise, only to be hit with the full force of the wind at the top. He squinted into the murky blizzard-like sky and thought he might have seen a yellowish blink of a man-made light.

Hope surged through his blood and powered him forward. Using his poles, he skated across the snow with his skis, aiming for the point at which he'd seen the light, praying it was a shed and Mitchell was safely inside, her bare hand warming.

If they had hurt her and dumped her over the side of the maintenance road, Remy didn't have a chance in hell of finding her until it was too late.

Chapter Eleven

A ROARING WAIL nudged Mitchell back to consciousness, and she blinked to clear her vision. For a moment she thought she'd gone blind, until a light flickered on and she could see the silhouettes of two men.

"Save your phone battery," a gruff voice said. "We might need it to find fuel for a fire."

"I should steal the bulb out of the light outside to replace the one in here that's burned out."

"Yeah, you do that." The man sitting on the other side of Flashlight Man snorted. "Got a ladder? Wanna stand out in that blizzard and unscrew a light bulb?"

"Fuck no." The beam swung her way. "How will we know when she's awake if we don't use the flashlight?"

Mitchell closed her eyes almost all the way, leaving just a slit so that she could watch what they were doing. Her arms were trapped together in front of her body, the sleeves of her jacket wrapped in duct tape. A dull ache pounded in her head.

"She'll be out for a while. She hit the ground pretty hard. Besides, she's tied up. What could she do, anyway?"

"Why didn't we just kill her and dump her over a cliff?" Flashlight man spat on the floor. "The snow would have buried her until spring."

"Rocco wanted her alive. He has plans for her."

The man with the flashlight clicked it off and chuckled. "Bet he plans on selling her to the highest bidder."

"Yeah. She should bring top dollar. She's in good shape. I saw her in the pool last night. Looks great in a bikini."

The light flashed on. "How long do you think we'll be holed up here?" Light blinked off.

"Too long, if you ask me. And it's getting colder. If this storm doesn't let up soon, it'll be morning before we can get out."

Again, the light came on. "Rocco ain't gonna like that. Too many eyes in the light of day. Someone might recognize him from his picture on TV."

"Good news is that if we can't get out because of the storm, Rocco can't fly out either. He'll be coolin' his heels in that hangar at the airport. Turn off that damned light."

Mitchell's heart skipped several beats. Rocco was in Vail.

The light blinked off. "Do ya think Joey made it back to the airport?" Flashlight man said into the dark.

"I think he had the toughest job of all of us. Attacking a SEAL, even if he's not expectin' it,

154

isn't something I'd wanna do."

"He was supposed to kill him and meet us here."

No. Mitchell refused to believe Remy was dead. But that didn't stop her chest from aching and her eyes burning with unshed tears. She focused on getting out of her current situation alive so that she could get back to Remy.

As far as she could tell, she was laying on the floor of what appeared to be an equipment shed littered with shovels, old snowmobile skids, a faded gas can, and a broken-down rescue basket. She guessed it was a shed on the ski slope. Thankfully, they hadn't made it off the mountain, and Rocco's orders weren't to kill her. He wanted her to suffer for breaking up his and Candy's human trafficking operation.

Unfortunately, just because they caught Rocco, didn't mean the NCIS stopped the flow of women being sold. Nor had they jailed the men or organizations who bought them to establish brothels for paying customers. The money was good. Rocco and Candy probably had a stash somewhere in a foreign bank with which they could restart the business.

While the light was off, Mitchell raised her arms and sank her teeth into the tape around her forearms. She managed to gnaw through one layer before the light flashed on again. She laid her arms down slowly, trying not to draw attention to herself.

"Bet Rocco's glad Candy's still in jail."

Flashlight Man shone the light into the far corner, running it along the wall to the other corner before he clicked it off. "You don't think he'll try to bust her out?"

"Hell, no. She jerked his chain every which way and acted like she ran the show. Rocco's probably glad she's out of the picture."

A long stretch of silence followed, and then the guy with the smart phone flashlight said, "This storm fuckin' sucks." The light blinked on and the man stood. "I'm gonna check outside. If we can see anything, I vote we get off this mountain while we can. I don't wanna get caught up here all night." He jerked open the door, and it slammed against the wall with the force of an arctic blast blowing though.

The wind chilled Mitchell, but gave her the distraction and noise she needed to tear through several more layers of the tape. Just a little more and—

"Shut the fuckin' door, dumbass." The other man lurched to his feet and shoved the door closed. "It's cold enough in here without you letting out any heat we generate."

"Did you see? Storm looks like it's easing up."

The flashlight shined into the other man's face and he raised his hand to block the light. "So?"

"So, with the headlight on the snowmobile, we should be able to drive down the mountain. Come on." Flashlight Man zipped the front of his jacket all the way up to his chin, reached down, and grabbed Mitchell's jacket, dragging her to her feet.

She slumped, pretending she was still out of it, falling like deadweight into Flashlight Man.

"Damn, woman. I know you're awake. Don't fuck with me." He backhanded her, sending her staggering across the cramped space. She tripped over the empty gas can and landed on her knees on the hard dirt floor. What the men couldn't see was that she'd broken through the last of the tape.

"Let's get out of here. I don't relish being caught here with the chick on our hands. Rocco's the one who was convicted. If anyone goes to jail for assaulting a fed, let it be him."

"Now you're talking." Flashlight Man shined the light toward her. "Get up, bitch." He kicked her hip.

She pretended to fall, landing on her side. Then she rolled over, caught Flashlight Man's legs between hers and twisted, sending him toppling to the ground.

Jumping to her feet, she plowed headfirst into the other man with her helmet, glad they hadn't seen fit to remove it. The hard plastic made a great battering ram and she used it to her best advantage, slamming the guy up against the wall.

He hit hard, but was so wrapped in cold weather padding, the blow didn't hurt him badly enough to knock him out.

Her only hope was to get out of the shed and

hide in the snowstorm.

"I wouldn't try it," said the man against the wall as he held her Glock aimed at her chest.

"I'm gonna kill that bitch." Flashlight Man stood, dripping blood from his nose, and lunged forward.

Mitchell sidestepped him and shoved him in the back, sending him straight into the other guy.

The gun went off with a blast that echoed, and Flashlight Man slumped to the ground.

"Fuck!" the other man yelled. "Look what you made me do. Fuck!"

Diving for the door, Mitchell yanked it open and would have made it out, but another loud bang echoed in the small confines of the shed, and heat slapped into her shoulder. Pain radiated through her chest and arms. She took one step and fell face-first into the snow, the icy flakes stinging her skin.

Though she tried to push to her knees, she couldn't make her arm work, and rolled to her side instead. She gazed up at a dingy yellow light blinking in the storm at one corner of the shed. Something warm and sticky slid across her skin. Was this it? Was she destined to die from a gunshot wound, her body buried in the snow until someone stumbled upon her?

Had Joey succeeded in killing Remy? Was he lying on the slope, being buried by the same heavy snowfall?

A tear slipped from the corner of her eye. Just one.

"You bitch! You made me kill him. I should fuckin' shoot you for that." He aimed her own gun at her head.

Anger knifed through her. These men hurt Remy. She couldn't leave him on the slopes to die, and she couldn't let these men get away with murder. Not only did she have to live to help Remy, she now knew where Rocco was. She had to stay alive long enough to tell someone.

Mitchell kicked hard and fast, her heavy ski boot slamming into the man's hand holding the gun. His wrist snapped and the gun flew out into the snow.

The man screamed and kicked hard, landing his boot in her rib.

Pain shot through her, but she wasn't done yet. She couldn't be.

The guy kicked again, and she grabbed his foot with her good hand and twisted.

He tripped over her body and landed on his broken wrist, screaming again. Rolling onto his side, he came up on his knees and clamped his good hand on her throat, squeezing hard.

Mitchell bucked and kicked, but couldn't throw off the heavier man. She couldn't let him win. Remy was somewhere on the mountain and she had to get back to him.

The yellow light faded to gray, and darkness threatened to extinguish it altogether.

No. She needed to get to Remy. She had to tell him…to tell him…that she loved him.

Remy skated across the knee-deep snow, focusing on that yellow light, now glowing brighter and brighter, like a beacon, drawing him near as if to say this is where he'd find Mitchell. And if he didn't?

He refused to think past reaching the light.

As he drew closer, the snow abated a little, and he could make out the shape of a building. The light was fixed to the outside of a maintenance shed. Still a football field distant, he picked up his heavy boots and forced his skis to slide through the snow, his calves and thighs burning from the effort.

A muffled bang alerted him to potential gunfire.

Please, not Mitchell.

He skied faster.

Suddenly, the door to the shed flew open and another shot rang out. A figure in a white jacket fell through and landed face-first in the snow.

Mitchell had been wearing a white jacket. A dark stain spread across the back of the white jacket. Was she dead? For a moment, she lay completely still. Then she rolled onto her back.

Remy couldn't get to her fast enough.

A big man lurched out into the snow, aiming a gun at her head.

Like watching a silent moving unfolding before him, Remy could do nothing to stop the man. His shouts were swallowed by the wailing wind.

Mitchell kicked her leg, caught the man's hand with the gun, and sent it flying through the air, and then he fell to the ground, rolled on top of her, and was choking her when Remy finally reached the two.

He yanked off the man and slammed his fist into the man's face hard enough that, even with his hands gloved, the punch made the man's head snap back and he staggered backward, landing on his ass in the snow.

"Remy?"

"I'm here, babe." Heart rate in overdrive, he squatted in the snow beside her. "Whatcha got there?" He wanted to unzip her jacket and get an idea of how bad her wound was, but the cold might kill her before the blood loss.

She coughed, and said in a scratchy voice, "I'm okay. And if you shoot that bastard, you won't hurt my feelings."

The man on the ground groaned and tried to crawl to where the other gun had landed in the snow.

Remy pulled his H&K .40 from his pocket and pointed it at the man. "Move, and I'll shoot you as a Christmas present to my girl."

The man lay still for a moment, and then flung himself toward the gun on the ground.

Remy pulled the trigger, hitting the man in the thigh.

He rolled onto his back, screaming in pain.

"Sweetheart, get my Glock, if you can." Mitchell's voice faded into a whisper Remy had to lean close to hear. "I like that gun."

Torn between getting her gun and slowing the blood loss, Remy remained at her side and pressed a hand to her wound, applying enough pressure to keep her from bleeding out. He debated moving her back into the building, but the reassuring rumble of an approaching vehicle made him decide to leave her there. Using his body to block the wind and driven snow, he kept a steady pressure on her wound.

Mitchell opened her eyes and gazed upward. "Before I pass out, you need to know."

"Whatever you have to say can wait. Conserve your energy."

She gripped his hand with her good one and held it with surprising strength. "Rocco's here."

Remy turned toward the shed. "Here?"

She smiled and closed her eyes. "Not here, but in Vail. He's at the airport, in one of the hangars."

Peeling off one of his gloves, he called Agent Thurmon and relayed the information.

"I'll send someone over there before anyone hears anything about what's going on here over the police scanner."

"What's your ETA? Mitchell's been shot."

"ETA, two mikes."

Two minutes later, the snow crawler and three snowmobiles stopped beside them. Emergency medical technicians unloaded equipment and converged on Mitchell. Within minutes, they had her covered in blankets, loaded into the crawler, an IV started, and a pressure bandage taped in place over the entry and exit point of her gunshot wound.

Another EMT administered aid to the man who'd shot Mitchell. Part of Remy wished he'd killed the man for hurting her. He hoped he'd have the opportunity to testify against the man in court, to ensure he served the maximum sentence for attempted murder.

Both patients were loaded into the crawler, and the dead man was loaded into one of the baskets pulled behind a snowmobile. The vehicles moved slowly back down the mountain in the blinding snow, careful not to drive too close to the edge of a drop off.

Remy sat between Mitchell and her captor, who'd been firmly strapped to the backboard. Remy held Mitchell's hand the entire trip down the mountain, where two ambulances awaited them at the base.

Mitchell blacked out on the trip down the mountain. When she was transferred to the ambulance, she gripped Remy's arm. "Make sure Rocco doesn't get away."

"What about you?"

She smiled. "I'm not going anywhere. Please, go with Agent Thurmon. I have to know Rocco is captured."

Remy reluctantly released her hand and watched as she was loaded into the ambulance, the door closing behind her.

"The county sheriff and five of his squad cars

are meeting me at the entrance to the airport. They're under strict radio silence. He notified them all by their cell phones. Are you going with me?"

"Mitchell wanted me to go along for the ride. She needs to know with absolute certainty that Rocco is captured and will not get away again."

"You can go along, but not armed."

"I can live with that." He handed over both his weapon, and the Glock he'd retrieved for Mitchell. "As long as you nail the bastard. And believe me, shooting him would be too good for his sorry ass."

"Let's do this."

Thurmon led Remy to a rental SUV.

The ski boots weighed him down. "You don't happen to have a spare pair of snow boots, do you?"

"No, but I have some gum boots in the back of the vehicle." Thurmon opened the back, dug out a pair of rubber boots, and handed them to Remy. "They won't keep your feet warm, but they aren't as heavy as the ski boots."

Remy quickly unbuckled the ski boots, dropped them in the back of the SUV, and pulled on the gum boots. He felt lighter, but Thurmon was right, his feet were already getting cold.

Within a few precious minutes, they drove out of the parking lot, headed for the Eagle County Airport. A quarter of a mile before they reached it, a sheriff's SUV stopped them.

"The Vail SWAT team was sent in to check

out the hangars. They've located Rocco." He held out a computer tablet with an aerial view of the buildings surrounding the flight line. Pointing at the one at the end of the row of privately owned hangars, he said. "He's in there."

"Does he know anyone is onto him?"

"I don't think so. He posted guards on the corners of the hangar building. It's the only building with guards standing out in the cold. SWAT is in place, and we have the roads out of the airport blockaded."

"What can we do to help?" Agent Thurmon asked.

The sheriff sighed. "We've been ordered to stay out of the way. The SWAT team has everything under control."

Remy stood in the middle of the road. He didn't like being on the periphery of the action with no say or control. But this operation wasn't his to run. The best he could do was wait for the SWAT team to do their job. Then he could go back to Mitchell and let her know Rocco was either captured, or dead.

"I don't like being on the outside, looking in," Thurmon commented, rubbing his gloved hands together for warmth.

"How long until they initiate contact?" Remy asked.

A loud boom sounded, and the earth shook beneath Remy's feet.

"I'd say they've initiated contact," the sheriff said.

Immediately, his radio crackled, and an excited voice came on. "Suspect got through and is headed your way in a black Ford Excursion!"

The sheriff waved his hands at the SUVs idling at the sides of the road. The drivers pulled their vehicles across the road, overlapping them to create even more of a barrier.

No sooner had they moved into place, a vehicle appeared, headlights on high beam, the lights reflecting off the barricading vehicles in the center of the road.

"They aren't slowing," Remy said, his muscles tensing.

"Get out of the vehicles," the sheriff yelled.

Doors opened and deputies bailed out and ran away from the barricade.

The big, black SUV slammed into the two vehicles, pushing them forward twenty feet. On impact, the airbags inside the Ford Excursion deployed, blinding the driver.

The doors burst open. Three men leaped out with automatic weapons and sprayed the immediate vicinity with bullets.

As soon as the doors opened, Remy dropped to the frozen ground. Without a gun, he couldn't defend himself and gritted his teeth at the lack.

"God damn!" Agent Thurmon dropped to the ground beside him, rolled onto his side, pulled out a Glock, and aimed at one of the shooters.

The sheriff and his men took cover behind whatever they could. Two of the deputies were hit, and lay bleeding on the ground.

"Here." The NCIS agent shoved Remy's H&K .40 at him. "Do what you can. It's a fuckin' bloodbath with those automatics."

Remy wished he had his H&K 416 rifle, but was happy he had something. Problem was, at that distance, he couldn't get a good shot. He had to move forward. "Cover me."

With random bursts from the automatic weapons, the gunmen peppered the ground surrounding the SUV, the shots reverberating in the cold air.

Remy would be taking a big risk. If he did nothing, the sheriff and his deputies would be killed. Remy low-crawled into a roadside ditch that provided some cover, but meant he had to stand to stay above the snow drifts. Hunkered low, he moved parallel to the firefight until he was perpendicular to the SUV. Then, crawling up the banks of the ditch, he lay in the foot-deep snow and lined his sights on the armed man taking cover behind the rear door of the SUV.

He breathed in and held the breath, caressed the trigger.

The bullet hit the man in the chest. He crumpled to the ground where he stood, his finger still squeezing the trigger of his automatic weapon, the barrel pointing at an angle. Several bullets hit the man taking cover behind the front door of the SUV. His knees buckled, and he fell to the ground screaming and cursing, still firing at the sheriff's vehicles and anything that moved.

Remy took him out with a single bullet,

hitting him in the head.

The gunman on the other side of the vehicle fired until he ran out of bullets. One of the sheriff's deputies, or the sheriff, took him out.

From where Remy lay, he could see a shadow hunkered low in the front passenger seat of the vehicle. Then a body tumbled out of the driver's seat, landing on the ground in a heap. The door closed and the vehicle shifted into reverse, its tires spinning on the icy pavement until they engaged, sending the Excursion backward and spinning around.

Remy shot at the front tires, hitting one.

The spinning vehicle careened out of control and rolled into the ditch, flipped, and landed upside down.

Lying still, Remy waited for the sheriff's deputies to move forward. Because he was farther forward than they were, he stayed put, not wanting them to mistake him for one of Rocco's men. But he kept a close watch on the upside-down vehicle. He wouldn't let Rocco escape. Not this time. The man's number was up.

Sheriff's deputies, the SWAT team, and ambulances converged on the downed officers, gunmen, and the wrecked Ford. Breathing deep to release adrenaline, Remy pocketed his weapon and stood. For the first time since the bullets began flying, he could feel the cold biting at his toes.

He joined Agent Thurmon on the pavement.

The agent handed him Mitchell's Glock.

"Here. I never should have taken away your guns."

Remy palmed the gun and then shoved it in his back waistband. "At least, you didn't hesitate to return one when I needed it."

"Figured we could use all the help we could get."

Two sheriff's deputies dragged a body out of the wrecked vehicle and up onto the pavement. "It's him, the man on the wanted poster. Rocco Hatch," one said.

The other straightened, his face grim. "He's dead. Broke his neck in the rollover. He wasn't wearing a seat belt."

Remy knelt beside the man who'd nearly succeeded in killing the woman he loved. Just to make sure, he touched his fingers to the man's neck. He couldn't feel a pulse, and the dirtbag's skin was already cooling in the frigid air. When he straightened, he stared across at Agent Thurmon. "Could you take me to the hospital?"

The man nodded. "Gladly."

Tired, his toes going numb, bruised from fighting bad guys, Remy felt a flood of relief wash over him. The hunt was over. Rocco wouldn't terrorize Mitchell ever again.

Chapter Twelve

MITCHELL OPENED her eyes and stared up at a bright florescent light hanging from a sterile white ceiling. Her body was draped in a heated blanket, instead of inside a dark, freezing shed, tied up and awaiting her fate at the hands of Rocco Hatch's henchmen.

"Hey, gorgeous."

At the sound of a deep voice, she turned her head and her chest filled with warmth.

Remy sat in a chair beside her hospital bed, wearing the sweatshirt he'd worn skiing. His hair was rumpled and he had a thick, black shadow of a beard. Though his eyes were bloodshot and he appeared a little worse for the wear, he was the most beautiful man she'd ever known.

"I'm not gorgeous. In fact, I imagine I look like a train wreck." She tried to raise a hand to brush the hair out of her face, but the one she lifted had an IV stuck in it.

Remy chuckled. "You look pretty good for a train wreck."

"I don't suppose you have a hairbrush or a toothbrush handy?"

"Let me check the bag the hotel sent over. I understand you refused to go into surgery until you had them promise to deliver some of your things."

"They brought it?" Mitchell had refused to let the nurses wheel her toward the operating room until she cajoled, begged, and pleaded for them to do one thing for her. She had them call the hotel staff and ask them to deliver the Christmas package she'd left on the desk in her room to the hospital for when she got out of recovery. Mitchell lifted her head and the room spun a little. "Whoa. I feel like I've been on an all-night bender."

"Pain meds and the effects of anesthesia will do that to you." Remy stood and smoothed the hair back from her face. "The doc said you're going to heal just fine."

"That son of a bitch hit me in my shooting arm."

"Yeah, but it was a clean shot, and didn't tear up the bone or muscles. EMTs were mostly concerned with your blood loss. The doctors here got that under control and gave you a few pints of refill. With a couple week's physical therapy, you'll be back to shooting bad guys." He crossed to a small cabinet and opened the door. Inside was a plastic bag. "This was the bag of things the hotel staff sent over."

"Could you bring it here, please?"

He did and laid it beside her on the bed. "What do you want first?"

"A nurse, and you out of here for a few minutes." She reached for the call button and pressed it. "Nothing personal, but I could use a little help cleaning up."

"I don't mind doing it."

"I thought a man liked a girl with a little mystery."

A soft knock on the door preceded the entrance of a nurse wearing cheerful scrubs with a pattern of Christmas trees and candy canes scattered across a bright green background. "Merry Christmas, you two. Is there something I can do for you?"

"Yes," Mitchell said. "Boot him out."

"Sir..."

"I know. I'm leaving. But not for long." He winked at Mitchell.

A simple gesture that set off those butterflies in her stomach. She wondered how many years they had to be together before the butterflies faded. Hopefully, never.

The nurse helped her to the bathroom where she used the facilities, washed her hands and face, and brushed her teeth. After escorting her patient back into the bed, the nurse brushed her hair and tucked the blanket back around her, adjusting the bed to a more comfortable sitting position. "Now you're perfect."

Mitchell didn't feel perfect, with her shoulder bandaged and a bruise on her cheekbone where she'd been backhanded by Flashlight Man.

"Will you help me with one more thing?" Mitchell asked before the nurse could leave.

"Certainly."

"There should be a gift bag in that plastic sack. Could you hand it to me?"

The nurse found the gift bag and set it beside her on the bed. "Is it for your fella?"

Mitchell's cheeks warmed. "Yes." God, she hoped he liked it. He'd done so much to make her Christmas special.

After a last glance at the readouts, the nurse left.

Before the door closed, Remy returned.

"Much better," he said, and sat in the chair beside her.

"Uh-uh. Not there." Mitchell scooted over and patted the bed. "Come here."

Remy's brows dipped. "Are you sure? Don't want to hurt you."

"Never more sure in my life. Get up here."

He eased onto the bed and smiled. "Merry Christmas."

"You, too." She handed him the bag. "I hope you like it."

Remy's frown returned. "You didn't have to get me anything."

She shook her head. "Yes, I did." Mitchell rested her hand on his leg while he pulled the tissue out of the bag, laying it on the chair beside him. "I wanted to give you something that says how much you mean to me, and how honored I am that you want me in your life."

Eyes wide, Remy pulled out the cat-o-nine-tails and laughed out loud. "Babe, I can't think of anything that says honor more than one of these."

"Crap." Mitchell's cheeks burned. "I forgot that was in there. Look for the box at the bottom. That's the real gift. The other was just for fun."

A grin spreading across his face, Remy set the cat-o-nine-tails on the bed, his chest shaking with residual laughter. "Wait'll the guys hear about that."

"You wouldn't!" Mitchell pressed her hand to her burning cheeks and held her breath while he surfaced the ring box and held it in his hand.

He glanced across at her. "Is this what I think this is?"

Mitchell nodded, worried when his brows dipped low and he didn't open the box.

He opened the box and stared down at the ring inside. "Mitchell." He slid off the bed. "I—"

Mitchell held up her hand, her heart pounding against her chest. "You don't have to keep it if you don't like it, and I'm not asking you to make a commitment, if you don't want to. Damn it, Remy! I love you, and wanted something that told you that I'll love you forever."

"But, Mitchell, sweetheart…" He backed away from the bed, digging his free hand into his pocket.

Her racing heart dove into her belly. She'd screwed it up. The man obviously wasn't ready for the next step in their relationship, and she'd pushed him too fast. She wouldn't be surprised if he walked—no, ran—out of the hospital room without saying goodbye.

"Oh, Remy, I'm sorry if I've ruined everything." Her breath caught, and she swallowed hard. "I just realized that you're everything I've ever wanted, even though I didn't know I wanted it. And forever isn't long enough to be with you. Please, don't leave me."

"Leave you?" He laughed, the sound somewhat choked as he dropped to his knees on the floor and gathered her hand in his. "Oh, baby, I'd never leave you. I set up this trip for one purpose and one purpose only. And I so wanted the moment to be special."

Mitchell's eyes misted and a tear trickled down her cheek. "And I ruined it."

"No, you made it perfect." He handed her small black box with a red ribbon wrapped around it. "I wanted it to be special when I asked you to marry me. Because, you see, I could not imagine my life without you in it."

Tears flowed in earnest now, and Mitchell brushed them aside. "Why?"

Remy opened the box and removed the diamond engagement ring. "Not exactly the response I'd hoped for, but at least it wasn't a 'no.'"

"I'm not a romantic." She waved a hand. "You know that."

"Don't worry, I'm good at that. Two romantics would make things a bit mushy all the time."

Mitchell laughed and hiccupped. "I'm not a girly-girl."

He slid the ring onto her left finger and kissed her. "You're a girl in all the important ways."

"You could do so much better than me."

He climbed on the bed beside her and carefully slid his arm around her. "On that subject, you're wrong. You are perfect to me, and I wouldn't have anyone else. I love that you're tough. It takes a strong woman to marry a SEAL. One who is independent, can take care of herself, and still find it in her heart to love him when he's there and when he's gone." He held her hand in his, looked straight into her eyes, and asked, "So, Mitchell Sanders, will you marry me?"

"You're sure you want me?"

"Never more sure of anything in my life." He kissed her lips and curled his hand around hers. "You're wearing my ring. I won't take it back. Please, say yes."

Her heart bursting with happiness, she flung her free arm around him and shouted, "Yes!"

As Remy held the woman he loved and promised to make her happy, he could hear applause and cheering in the hallway, and the excited chatter of nurses all saying, "She said 'yes.'"

Remy couldn't remember a prouder, happier day in his life. He knew marriage wouldn't always be sunshine and roses, but he was a SEAL and all SEALs knew...

The only easy day was yesterday.

The End

About the Author

Elle James *also writing as Myla Jackson* spent twenty years livin' and lovin' in South Texas, ranching horses, cattle, goats, ostriches and emus. A former IT professional, Elle is proud to be writing full-time, penning intrigues and paranormal adventures that keep her readers on the edge of their seats. Now living in northwest Arkansas, she isn't wrangling cattle, she's wrangling her muses, a malti-poo and yorkie. When she's not at her computer, she's traveling, out snow-skiing, boating, or riding her ATV, dreaming up new stories.

To learn more about Elle James and her stories visit her website at http://www.ellejames.com.

To learn more about Myla Jackson visit her websites at www.mylajackson.com

SEAL's
Seduction

New York Times & USA Today Bestselling Author

ELLE JAMES

SEAL'S SEDUCTION

TAKE NO PRISONERS

BOOK #6

ELLE JAMES

New York Times & USA Today
Bestselling Author

Chapter One

TWO MILES AWAY from its target location, the Black Hawk helicopter slowed and hovered thirty feet off the ground. The whirling blades stirred the sultry night heat of Somalia.

Dustin Ford, nicknamed Dustman by his team, was first out, fast-roping to the ground. As soon as he hit the dirt, he ran to the two o'clock position to establish his section of the perimeter, his M4A1 aimed out into the dry foliage, his night vision goggles in place as he scanned for any heat signatures in the area.

The satellite images had pinpointed the Somali rebel camp at two miles to the south of where they'd landed. Even before the last man hit the ground, Dustin took point, moving quietly through the night.

Orders from above were to neutralize the rebels and rescue the American aid workers who had been held captive in an attempt to extort money from the U.S. government for their return.

With Irish on his right, Gator on his left and Tuck at his back, he'd be first to make contact. Intel estimated twenty rebel fighters, armed with whatever weapons they had collected. They would put up a fierce resistance…if the SEAL team lost the element of surprise early on. But Dustin's team was trained to get in and get out with minimal effort and loss of American lives.

As they neared the camp, Dustin could make out three blurry green heat signatures of sentries spread out fifty feet apart on the perimeter of the camp. He figured there were more on the other side.

Big Bird, Fish, Swede, Nacho and Rider fanned out to either side. While they moved into place to take out the sentries farther away, Dustin and his crew held fast, waiting for their cue to move in and silently dispatch the camp guards.

"In position," Big Bird said in Dustin's ear. Knives drawn, the team moved in. Before the guards knew what hit them, they were dispatched and lying silently in the dirt, their terrorist days done.

A sharp report of gunfire pierced the silence. A shout rose from one of the five tents, and terrorists wielding semi-automatic rifles and AK-47s rushed out of four of the five tents.

The SEAL team had the advantage of night vision goggles. One by one, they picked off the terrorists until the last one fell.

Dustin ducked low and ran toward the one tent no gunmen had emerged from. Other members of his team rushed the other tents and cleared them. More gunfire erupted and the usual confusion of battle ensued.

As he neared the exterior, Dustin shouted in Arabic for anyone inside the tent to come out. At first, he didn't hear anything. Then quiet sobbing came from inside. Dustin nodded to Gator, the big Cajun, who stood close to the entrance of the tent, while Dustin rounded to the rear.

When Gator repeated the Arabic command, Dustin drove his knife into the canvas and ripped an opening of his own.

A woman's scream filled the air. A dark-skinned Somali, his eyes rounded, held the American woman with a knife to her throat. He shouted in Arabic, "I will kill her."

Dustin eased forward, his hands out to the side, speaking in Arabic, "Put the knife down and we will let you live." While he had the Somali's attention, Gator slipped through the front flap and attacked the man from behind.

The terrorist fell forward, dead with a knife to the base of his skull, severing his brain stem.

The woman he'd held captive scrambled through the opening, her eyes wide, sobs shaking her body.

Dustin grabbed her and held her tight. For a woman in her late fifties, she fought like a wildcat, kicking and screaming, her fingernails slashing at his face.

"Martha!" he said, his voice stern, breaking through her crazed attempt at escape. "I'm an American, here to take you home."

He had to repeat himself several times before he got through to her and she sagged against him, her body spent, her sobs fading to silent tears. She clung to him for a moment then pushed away.

"John." She dropped to the floor beside the man lying on a grass mat, his eyes closed.

"Is he dead?" Gator asked.

Dustin squatted beside the man and pressed two fingers to the base of his throat. A weak, but steady pulse pushed back against his fingertips. "He's alive, but in bad shape. You take Martha. I'll get John."

Martha stumbled to her feet, swayed and would have fallen if Gator hadn't been there to scoop her up in his arms.

Dustin bent toward John and draped his body over his shoulder, then stood and exited through the front flap, held open by Irish.

"Need a hand?" Irish asked.

"I've got him."

The whop-whop of rotor blades filled the air. The sting of dust and flying debris whipped up into Dustin's face as he hurried toward the Black Hawk, depositing his charge on the floor of the craft. Fish bent over the man and went to work establishing an IV drip. Both John and Martha were suffering from severe dehydration and malnutrition from the month of captivity they'd endured with the Somali rebels, but they'd live, now that they were on their way home to the States.

Dustin glanced around at his teammates. All were present and accounted for. Mission accomplished, with no casualties except for those terrorists who would never terrorize another soul.

After they boarded the C-130 to take them

home, Tuck reported in with headquarters back in Little Creek, Virginia. When he came back to check on the team, he pulled Dustin aside. "As soon as we get back, you're to pack up and head to Texas."

Dustin's stomach took a dive to his kneecaps. "Why? What happened?"

"Your father had a heart attack. You'll be on emergency leave for a couple weeks."

"Jenna Turner, reporting live to you from a normally quiet street on the south side of Waco." Jenna faced the camera, holding the microphone in front of her mouth. Her pulse pounded and her hand shook slightly, but she forced herself to be calm and report the news as unbiased and composed as she could. "It's been four hours since Frank Mitchell barricaded himself in his mother's home, threatening to kill the elderly woman if anyone tried to come in after him." Toby, her cousin and cameraman, moved in a slow arc, recording behind her the modest white clapboard house with the old fashioned, metal awnings and peeling paint.

Jenna continued her monologue, "Our sources tell us Mitchell is wanted on several counts of armed robbery, assault, selling methamphetamines and resisting arrest. He could be under the influence of the drugs he deals and is considered a threat to his elderly parent."

The camera angled back toward her. "The Waco PD hostage negotiator has been on scene from the beginning, but nothing has changed in the past four hours." Except the fact her feet were killing her in her high-heeled boots, and she hadn't made it to a bathroom in hours. She regretted downing the fully leaded—sugar and caffeine-loaded—Dr. Pepper over an hour ago. If things didn't get hopping soon, she'd knock on a neighbor's door and ask to use their facilities.

"Jenna! Check it out. The SWAT team is headed in," Toby called out from behind the camera. He aimed his lens at the black armored van pulled to a stop two houses down from where Mitchell holed up. Men poured out, dressed in black uniforms, with olive drab bulletproof vests buckled in place over their chests.

Jenna's pulse leaped. Holy shit, this was it! This was her big chance to make it onto the national news. Alongside raging fires sweeping across California and hurricanes in the gulf, hostage situations ranked right up there and she was here, on the scene, camera ready. She held the microphone away from her mouth and whispered loud enough Toby could hear, "Are you getting this?"

"Damn right I am."

"We're here at the scene," Jenna said into the microphone. "The SWAT team has arrived, and they're surrounding the house."

"Ma'am." A police officer blocked Jenna's

view. "You'll have to back away from the house."

"But…" Jenna's pulse quickened and she stood on her toes to see past the policeman.

"I'm sorry. The chief insists all civilians remove themselves to a block away, in case shit hits the fan."

Members of the SWAT team took up positions around the house, poised to launch their attack and the big police officer had his hand in front of the damned camera.

Jenna dug her heels into the pavement. "I'm a reporter." She dug her press identification card out of her pocket and waved it in his face. "I have a right to be here."

The officer shook his head and spread his arms wide as if he would herd her away like a stray calf. "The chief said all civilians, including the press. It's for your own safety."

"What if I choose to accept the risk?"

"That doesn't mean squat to the chief. Off you go now, or I'll have to arrest you for interfering in a police operation."

"Damn!" This was her chance to show her boss at the station she could handle the intense and gritty situations.

Toby backed up, lowering his camera to catch what he could beneath the officer's arm. "Come on, Jenna. Let's do as the officer asks."

"But it's happening here and now. If we leave, we lose this opportunity."

Toby hooked her arm and dragged her down the street. "It's okay. We'll get a shot at it again."

He leaned close to her. "You're wasting time. Come on. I have another idea."

Biting down on her lip, Jenna allowed Toby to drag her down the street. As soon as the police officer turned his back, Toby snagged Jenna's arm and yanked her between two houses.

They backtracked to a deserted house catty-corner to the one under siege. Toby fished a metal file out of his front pocket and would have jammed it into the lock.

Jenna laid a hand on his arm and shook her head. "It's open." She gave the door a slight shove and it swung inward. The interior was empty, all furniture gone, and no drapes in the window. Old, broken, vinyl blinds hung in the windows, some open, others closed.

Toby gestured with his camera toward a staircase. "Ladies first."

Jenna scampered to the top and hurried for a front window, thanking her stars for her cousin's ingenuity. Now if they could keep from being arrested for breaking and entering, they might have a shot at catching the hostage crisis on video.

The little house had a single room at the top of the stairs, a loft with two gables protruding out over the roof. Jenna opened the cheap blinds and peered out.

For a moment she thought she might have missed the show. Nothing moved. She couldn't see the SWAT team and the police had all backed up, positioned behind the relative security of their patrol cars.

"I have a clear view from here," Toby called out. He'd parted the blinds over the gabled window and stuck his camera lens through the gap. Kneeling on the floor, he gazed into the viewfinder. "Nothing's happening."

"Do you think they're already inside?" Jenna asked.

"No. If they had made their move, the rest of the cops hanging around would be a little more agitated. Right now, the police are pointing their weapons at the house."

"Then let's do this." Her heart racing, Jenna switched on her microphone. "This is Jenna Turner, reporting from the scene of a hostage crisis in Waco. The SWAT team has arrived and is in position."

"There they go," Toby whispered, excitedly.

Jenna stared through the blinds as half a dozen SWAT team policemen stormed through the front door.

Though muffled by the glass in the windows, the distinct pop-pop sound of gunfire could be heard, followed by shouts. A window exploded near the front of the house and a man Jenna assumed was Mitchell fell out on the ground and rolled to his feet, pistol in both hands.

"He's on the ground." Jenna jerked the blinds up to better see what was going on.

The officers behind their vehicles opened fire, but not before Mitchell let loose a round of bullets, some hitting the police cars.

Her voice shaking, Jenna spoke into her mic, "Mitchell is out of the house, firing at the police behind the barricade. He's been hit! But he's not going down without a fight."

As the bullets slammed into the man, he jerked, his hands rising, the guns with them. He dropped to his knees, still firing, only this time into the air.

The plink of glass breaking was quickly followed by a stinging sensation against her right temple. "Ouch." Jenna ducked to the side, refusing to look away from the scene unfolding.

Then it was over. Mitchell collapsed onto the front lawn of his mother's house and lay still.

The SWAT team emerged. One man had his arm around an old woman, helping her through the door and out into the open, shielding her from the sight of her son lying on the ground.

"Show's over. Let's transmit this to the station." Toby straightened and glanced her way, his brow furrowing. "Jenna, what the hell?"

She dragged her gaze from what was going on below and glanced at Toby. "What?"

"Your face is bleeding."

She raised her hand to where she could feel a slight stinging sensation and encountered warm wetness. "What's this?"

"Sweetheart, it's blood."

Jenna glanced at her fingers, covered in her own blood. Her knees weakened, and her head spun. "I think I've been shot."

Then the bright Texas sun outside blinked

out.

Other Titles by Elle James

Brotherhood Protector Series
Montana SEAL (#1)
Bride Protector SEAL (#2)
Montana D-Force (#3)

Take No Prisoners Series
SEAL's Honor (#1)
SEAL's Desire (#2)
SEAL's Embrace (#3)
SEAL's Obsession (#4)
SEAL's Proposal (#5)
SEAL's Seduction (#6)
SEAL's Defiance (#7)
SEAL's Deception (#8)
SEAL's Deliverance (#9)

SEAL of my Own Series
Navy SEAL Survival (#1)
Navy SEAL Captive (#2)
Navy SEAL To Die For (#3)
Navy SEAL Six Pack (#4)

Thunder Horse Series
Hostage to Thunder Horse (#1)
Thunder Horse Heritage (#2)
Thunder Horse Redemption (#3)
Christmas at Thunder Horse Ranch (#4)

Covert Cowboys Inc Series
Triggered (#1)
Taking Aim (#2)
Bodyguard Under Fire (#3)
Cowboy Resurrected (#4)
Navy SEAL Justice (#5)
Navy SEAL Newlywed (#6)
High Country Hideout (#7)
Clandestine Christmas (#8)

Billionaire Online Dating Series
The Billionaire Husband Test (#1)
The Billionaire Cinderella Test (#2)

Devil's Shroud or Deadly Series
Deadly Reckoning (#1)
Deadly Engagement (#2)
Deadly Liaisons (#3)
Deadly Allure (#4)
Deadly Obsession (#5)
Deadly Fall (#6)

Lords of the Underworld
Witch's Initiation (#1)
Witch's Seduction (#2)
The Witch's Desire (#3)
Possessing the Witch (#4)

Printed in the USA
CPSIA information can be obtained
at www.ICGtesting.com
LVHW012038080824
787734LV00008B/294